You are
loved

Blossom

By Cathy Jackson

Edited by Jennifer Harshman, Harshman Services

Cover design by Matthew Jackson

Acknowledgements

I want to thank GOD. Without Him, this story wouldn't be. I thank Him for teaching me and leading me every day.

Matthew Jackson, you are my heart and my life. Your encouragement has brought this book to life. Thank you for being my husband.

Connor, Ian, Jessa and Joseph, you are all my lights. I am so happy that each of you have been placed in my life. I love you all very much.

Jennifer Harshman of Harshman Services. I cannot express my gratitude. You continue to take a chance on me.

Opal Campbell, Videos by O. Your video graphics of Blossom are more than I could ever ask for. Thank you for all that you do!

John Wells. Thank you for being the face of John Westerling. My truest and most sincere thanks to you.

Bella Garcia and Casey Bond. Thank you for your encouragement, insight and some last minute edits.

Authors and Bloggers, your acceptance of who I am and what I write make you all golden in my book. I truly am thankful for each and every one of you.

Reader, this book has been a labor of love that I hope will encourage and inspire you. You are the ones who will make this book more than what I could ever make of it myself.

For Mom…

Chapter 1 "Letters From The Sky" – Civil Twilight

From the Journal of John Westerling
November 20th
My Wedding Day

Being a Child of God, for me, takes a lot of faith. So many things in my life have happened without me knowing why but trusting in the Lord that everything would be alright. I have been told I have a great faith but I don't know about that. I try to be a good man, trust in the Lord and do what he asks me without question. The few times I haven't done what He wanted ended catastrophically. Free will is my biggest asset and my greatest hindrance. Sometimes I wish I didn't have the luxury of free will so that I could always do what my Lord asks.

If I hadn't listened to Him, I wouldn't be standing here. The hand in mine was so trusting. The body belonging to it was mine, as mine was now hers. The smile on her beautiful face was almost too much for me to behold. I know what the angels must look like as I looked to my new wife. She is the loveliest woman I have ever seen.

Phoenix was nervous, and her hands were slick with moisture as they held mine. Her smile was a tenuous one even though she said she loves me.

There will be so many issues that we will have to work through now that our marriage has begun. Her dead husband both mentally and physically abused her. I could have killed him. Charles wasn't a nice man—not that I ever met him. But his treatment of my new wife was unconscionable. I know I should forgive him and it would be so easy now. I just can't bring myself to do so. Charles had driven himself off of a bridge just outside of town in a drunken stupor. With his death, Phoenix Swartz, now Phoenix Westerling, could finally heal and start blooming. Her bud had been held too tight for so long but on her own she had begun to open. Soon she would blossom and I would be there to see that. It would be a privilege to walk through the fire with my new wife.

We had come so far from when we first met. She would shy away from me, from my touch. I didn't know why then. Was she shy? Nervous around men? Not comfortable with strangers? Now I knew it was all of the above. And who could blame her after Charles? To Phoenix, every man was a Charles.

But by God's Grace, we became acquaintances, then friends, and then affianced. I had learned to read some of her moods and know some of her favorite things. There were so many things I knew about my new wife and so many more things I had yet to learn. But I had my whole life and I am a very patient man. I had to be to come this far.

My Pastor, Brice, had spoken and I had been listening to him, but my focus had been on my new bride. My love for her was more than I ever knew except for the love I had for Anna, my daughter from a previous marriage. Anna and Phoenix were now my world and I would do anything to keep them both safe.

Our first kiss as man and wife was more than I could ever imagine any kiss to be. Before now I was so chaste with Phoenix. Her cheeks and a few kisses on the forehead were the only places that received my lips. But now I could kiss her anywhere, everywhere I wanted because she was mine. You hear about the most magnificent, most engaging kisses on television and in movies. Their description is so rich in telling but the kiss that Phoenix and I exchanged was a kiss beyond words. I had to hold back an emotion I had never felt before, even for my first wife Catriona.

The taste of my new wife was still on my lips as we turned as one to face our friends and family. Restraining myself from licking the taste of her from them, I stepped closer to my Phoenix. I wanted the taste of her on my lips forever. She was sunshine and beauty, softness and love. But I also knew Phoenix was broken and skittish, even toward me. I try not to show the hurt I feel when she looks at me as if I were Charles. Sometimes when she thinks I am not looking at her I see her watching me. Often in wonder, sometimes in fear. I act like I don't see it, but I do. She doesn't mean to treat me that way, I don't even think she realizes that she does it. After five years with her previous husband who put her through a living hell, I can't blame her for the things she does. I love her.

The wedding party afterwards at the church with our family and friends was larger than I anticipated. Phoenix was so shy and stood behind me through it. Well, most of it. When I took her in my arms for our dance, I felt the proudest man alive. Her curves fit into mine as if we were made for one another. Even though I am a head taller than my new wife. She wasn't graceful on the dance floor, but I made her shine during our dance. Early in the dance she brought her feet to mine and I guided her. A privilege I will have the rest of our lives.

We left early, leaving Anna with Missy LeFevre, her Sunday School teacher. Missy has cared for my daughter almost since she was born. Anna is in good hands and I love her with my entire heart.

We took my truck back here to my house to pick up our things. She had left her things packed there from her last visit. I had picked her up before we came through the door and carried her over the threshold. My lips met hers as we walked through and I had to pull myself from her. If I had my way I would skip the drive to the inn. My new wife and I would enjoy our first moments together in my room. But we won't.

I'm not sure why but in my truck Phoenix had moved over to the door and eyed me on the drive back to my house. She was tense. I pretended not to notice as she sat from me. Even when I laid my hand where I usually did, as she needed to hold my hand as I drove, Phoenix didn't take it. At one point I could feel her looking at it, but she never made a move to hold it.

Phoenix is moving toward my room—our room now—and I can hear her trepidation. I would never do anything to hurt the woman I would give my life for, but I know she is afraid. I have to do everything I can to reassure her. My goal is that one day she doesn't look at me in fear but in love. I know she sees Charles when she looks at me, but I have to show her John. I am her husband now and the care and devotion I have for her will win her to me.

I hope.

***

I didn't know what to pack when I put together my suitcase for the honeymoon with my new husband. Lacy things were foreign to me and feminine looking items only served to put me off. Charles had never said anything about them and being raised with a brother did make me a sort of tomboy. Would John expect to see me in delicate things? I hoped not because they terrified me. It was just the unfamiliarity of the objects that intimidated me.

Holding the case in my hand, making my way to John's room, I felt so self-conscious. My palms wouldn't stop sweating! No matter how many times I rubbed them on my jeans they would immediately drench with sweat. My nerves were running overtime as I moved through the hall.

The first boyfriend I had was more of an expedition into the land of what I thought was love. That expedition only ended in heartache and pain. My first husband, Charles, was what I thought the man of my dreams. He was everything I thought he wasn't. Touching my back and the scars I knew I would carry for the rest of my life, they were a constant embarrassing reminder of Charles.

John Westerling was the first man I knew I ever truly loved. From the moment we met he began empowering me to be stronger than I was. He encouraged me and slowly I began to open up to the world. Still reclusive to almost anyone but him and Anna, I still had a long way to go. His touch to me had only ever been in love and never in anger. His words to me had always been spoken in love and my life was beginning to be everything it needed to be because he was in it.

In the doorway of his room—our room now—I saw him kneeling against his bed. His forehead was resting on his folded hands and I could see his lips moving. He looked so peaceful. Not wanting to bother him, I waited. My other hand went to the handle of my suitcase and I leaned against the doorway.

My husband was a little over six foot with dark brown almost midnight hair. His grey eyes could harden with rage or soften with love. Strong, singular features in his face made him even more physically handsome. And he was built! The corded muscles ran through his entire body and the raw power behind his strength was massive. I could stand there all day and watch him praying.

His head came up and he blinked as he looked to me. The mouth I had seen so many times set into a determined line and his eyes narrowed in on me. Standing up straight, I forced a smile. I loved him with my whole heart and this time we had together I wanted to be special to him. If mind reading was a thing, I would definitely want that so I knew what to do to please him.

Pushing himself off the floor, he stood straight and smiled now at me. I relaxed a little.

"Hello, wife. You look beautiful. Do you have everything you need?"

The words my husband had spoken made me glow inside and my smile relaxed on my face. A greeting, a compliment, and concern over what I needed. More things that made him so different from Charles.

"Yes. I…" The suitcase hit the floor softly and I heard a wooden thump. My hands came to my jeans, drenched again. "I think so. When I packed, I wasn't really sure what to bring so I just…" My words trailed off as I saw him pick up a suitcase twice as big as mine. John Westerling did not pack lightly.

"It will only be a couple of days and if we need anything while we are gone we'll just stop to pick it up." The smile on his face was a lazy one as he looked to me. Moving to me, he bent down and picked up my suitcase.

"What are you doing?"

"I'm going to carry our things to my truck then I am going to come back for my bride." He was already moving to the front door and I followed him. "I'll be a moment."

John carried the things to the back seat and set them inside. I saw him open the passenger side door, then lean in and turn on the truck. I grabbed my coat and held it in my hand. November was wrapping up and the air was nippy. He shivered as he walked back into the house. "Are you ready, my love?"

Nodding, I began to put on my coat but felt it moved from my hands. Immediately it was laid on my shoulders and I slid my arms into the holes. A hand turned me and swiftly the buttons were done. Both hands came to my shoulders and John laid his forehead against mine. His eyes closed and his lips moved.

"John?"

"I want to do this right with you, Phoenix. I am trying so hard to be the man you need." The sound of his voice tore at my heart and I brought my hands around him.

"You are everything I need. Everything." My toes pushed off the ground and I kissed his forehead.

The forehead pushed lightly against mine. "I want you."

Those three words had me instantly tensing and I had to restrain myself from pulling back from my husband. My tear ducts filled and I watched him warily.

John's eyes fluttered to me and then closed. "Be completely humble and gentle; be patient, bearing with one another in love. Make every effort to keep the unity of the spirit through the bond of peace." Hard grey eyes met mine now and his hands grasped mine. "We're married now, Phoenix."

The words dropped like lead into my soul. Did that mean he could do whatever he wanted to do to me? Like Charles? I shook my head and tried to pull my hands from his.

His hands slid out of mine and came softly to my cheeks. He leaned back to look into my eyes. The pads of his thumbs came to my lips as did his eyes. "I'm not him, my love. I'm not Charles. I won't take you like he did. Ever." He looked to me now. "Tonight or whenever you would like us to be together, I want you to be the one to initiate everything."

My curiosity was piqued and I tilted my head a little. I forgot about my fear of him. "Initiate..?"

"Yes. Everything that happens between us will be of your choosing and of your own free will. I want you to be the one to guide me in the bedroom." He blushed. I had never seen John Westerling blush! "At least for a while." His hands dropped to mine and his eyes looked at them. "I have a feeling I may want to eat… a lot of cheesecake with you, Mrs. Westerling."

Ah ha! When had said that earlier it *was* what I thought. I was sure of it. Heat came to my cheeks and I bit my lip as my eyes found the floor.

"And I want to do that, too." Didn't I? Yes. Yes, I did, but I was so afraid he would be another Charles. My eyes found his and my eyebrows knitted.

"I want to see what your lip tastes like when you bite it. It must be wonderful. You do it so often around me."

"I only do that because... I really don't know why I do that. It just feels right." I let go of my husband's hands and waved one through the air. As it went around, I felt John's arms come under me and lift me up. "What are you doing?"

John began moving through the house and out the door, pulling it closed with his foot behind him. "Practicing."

My arms were around his neck and l looked to him. "Practicing? For what?"

His head shook back and forth, a secret smile on his face. "I'm not telling. You'll just have to see."

"John Westerling. Man of secrets. Are there any more secrets I should know about, husband?" His eyes met mine and hardened as they assessed me. I gulped and moved in the seat he had set me in A feeling of being stalked came to me again. Alternately it frightened and attracted me.

"There is still so much we don't know about one another, Phoenix. So many things we have yet to explore together. But our love will see us through."

My door shut and I watched John move aroun the truck. Once he had climbed in and buckled, we pulled out of the driveway and he reached for my hand. I moved back toward the door and looked ou the window.

Silence reigned in the cab for a few moments.

"Phoenix?" My eyes moved to my husband. "When we left the wedding and we got into the truck you have backed away from me. You did so just now." His soft grey eyes flickered to mine. "Would you tell me why?"

Swallowing the lump that formed in my throat, I grabbed my seat belt. I didn't want to tell John why I was both mentally and physically moving away from him.

"We're in this together. I can't help you if you don't tell me how."

The gentle coaxing in his tone had a tear falling from my eye. I wiped at it and looked out the window. The lump in my throat had gotten bigger. Tracing the condensation on my window, I tried to speak. Finally, I could talk through lump in my throat. "Charles promised me a paradise vacation for our honeymoon. Instead he…" Two tears trailed down my cheek and I put the back of my hand against my mouth, "in the back of the limo… I thought he would be different, that he would be gentle." I looked to him. "His hand came over my mouth, he pushed me against the seat, and tore my dress in his haste to have what he wanted. It was painful…" Clearing my throat, I went on. "When he was done, I just remember being shocked. This wasn't the man I married it was someone else. Someone cruel and dangerous." My hands came to my face, shame washing over me.

The truck came to a stop and I heard a door open. Another one opened too. "I'm sorry, Phoenix." John's unbuckled my seat belt, his arms came around me and I wailed louder as he picked me up.

"I didn't know."

His hand stroked my hair softly and the other one came to my cheek, his thumb caressing my lip. "He shouldn't have done that to his wife. I will never hurt you, my love." I heard him sigh loudly. "I didn't mean to bring that up."

Cradled in his arms now, he began to rock me. Slowly I began to bring myself under control and the crying eased off. "You didn't know. I don't mean to pull away from you. I'm so sorry."

His hand came under my chin and my head was lifted to look into his eyes. "You never have to apologize to me. I love you. There will be many demons we will have to face together and I want to slay them with you."

Nodding my head, I was trapped in his gaze.

"Will you let me help you move passed the things that haunt you, my love?"

"Yes." That one word was said on a sigh and I saw his lips curve into a smile. "Yes, I will."

"Good." His lips touched mine briefly, not giving me any time to savor them. I pouted but John wasn't paying attention. Buckling my seat belt, he climbed back in and we started down the road. His hand came to me. "May I?"

My hand moved to his almost on its own and John clasped it. A small part of my soul breathed a sigh of relief. Moving over in the seat, against the console that separated us, I looked to my new husband. "Thank you."

His glance to me was almost immediate and his hand tightened a little on mine. "For what?"

"Being so patient with me. Loving me. Pick one." I closed my eyes. A tiredness moved over my soul and the ease was back between us. "How long to the inn?"

"Should only take a couple of hours. You didn't want to be too far from Anna and, truth be told, neither did I. Since she's been born, except for being with Catriona, I haven't been away from her too long. Missy and Dale are good people, Anna is going to have a good time. Are you tired?"

"Just a little." I tried to relax in my seat but I was too aware of John and what lay ahead at the end of the drive. "John?"

"Hm?"

"What if I… can't? Tonight." My eyes opened and I looked at him. A muscle ticked in his jaw and his eyes narrowed at the road.

"Then we will both have to be more patient with one another." He sighed loudly and the sound almost reverberated frustration. "We have the rest of our lives, Phoenix."

I sighed too. The thought of being with John was perfect but what if I couldn't bring myself to trust him with my body? "I want to."

"I know you do. Why don't you rest? I'll let you know when we get there."

"Alright." I could already feel myself drift off, lulled by the sound of John's voice and the motion of the truck. Just before I felt myself pulled under by sleep, I whispered, "I love you, John Westerling."

Just before I dropped off, I heard his reply. "I love you too, Phoenix Westerling."

Chapter 2 "Wait" - M83

The inn was exactly like John and I discussed when we looked at it online. Entering our suite, I was amazed by the size. John carried our things to the bedroom. A large bed sat in the middle of the room and I couldn't help but stare at it. I heard John put our things in the closet area. Trying not to panic, I brought myself to the wall.

"Phoenix?'

John was coming at me now and I tried not to shake my head. What was wrong with me? Before we were married the idea of being with John was almost consuming and now I couldn't do it.

"Breathe. My love, you're hyperventilating."

I was? Concentrating, I realized my breath was coming out in short pants. John's hands were warm on my shoulders.

"No." Moving from him, I made my way out the door out onto a private balcony and grabbed the almost frozen railing. Trying to concentrate on the surroundings, I breathed in great gulps of cold air. Hearing John come outside, I focused on the horizon.

"Phoenix, are you alright?"

Shaking my head back and forth once, I concentrated on spacing my breaths. The view was gorgeous and the thought to keep focusing on that was paramount.

"Is there anything I can do?"

My head jerked back and forth once then stopped. My breathing had evened out but I still couldn't turn to John. Hearing him move, I stood still. *Please don't touch me.*

Blossom

Out of the corner of my eye I saw him on the other side of the balcony. "I picked this place for you. It's supposed to be in balance with calming colors and presence. There are many amenities that could do, if you want. We don't have to be in the room at all unless it's to sleep."

Turning my head to him, my eyebrows knitted together. "You picked this place for me?"

John looked at me as he leaned against the rail. "Yes. I wanted you to be pampered and feel peace."

"I don't think I can ever feel at peace, John." The horizon captured my attention and I sighed. The view was gorgeous.

"Can I..?" John took a step toward me and stopped.

Closing my eyes, I nodded my head.

He walked slowly toward me and held out his arms. Slowly they slid around me from behind and I held myself still. His chin rested on my head and I heard him exhale. "Nothing has to happen. It's just you and me. This is our honeymoon but we can do this any way you want." I felt his chest rise as he took a breath. Feeling his head lift, he placed a kiss on top of it. "I love you."

I knew he loved me. And I loved him. I had said that once. I love you but I couldn't bring myself to say it again. "I know."

For a while we stood there in the cold John's arms wrapped around me. Admittedly, I felt... safe. They were so big with a restrained power that I knew could overwhelm me. Oddly enough I knew they wouldn't.

Maybe...

"Do you want anything? Look around? Hungry?"

John's concern touched me. "No. I like it just like this. Can we stand here for a bit?"

"Of course." Another kiss to my head and I closed my eyes. Shivering, I brought John's arms closer around me. The body heat being thrown off him enveloping me in the cold. I loved John Westerling. I loved his daughter and the new life we were going to build.

"I am getting a little hungry. On the menu is an appetizer with cheeses, crackers, little assorted things. I'm going to order one for us to share." His arms slipped slowly from around me and he turned to go inside.

Watching the horizon for a second longer, I turned to see John on the phone and speaking softly. His head shook once and I heard him say no. What was that about? He hung up the phone and turned to his suitcase.

Wandering inside, I shut the door and took one step inside. "Everything alright?"

"Yes." He was laying out his things in an arrangement.

"I heard you say no."

"They offered me a bottle of wine. I didn't want any." Turning to me, his smile was back along with a set of bath items in his hands. He began to move to the bath and I followed.

Charles, my first husband was an alcoholic. I knew John wasn't but he had also told me he did partake but not often. Because of Charles I didn't drink alcohol at all. "Why? It's our honeymoon."

Blossom

He set the things in his hands onto the sink counter and turned to me. "I didn't order the wine because it is our honeymoon." Coming up to me, he took my shoulders into his hands. "It would take quite a bit to dull my senses, but I want to be completely alert for you. This is as much about you as it is for me. To order it would be bringing…memories into our time and I don't want that."

Sighing, I nodded my head. There was something else John was not telling me, I was sure of it, but I wouldn't push it. "That was very thoughtful. Thank you."

The knock at the door surprised me.

"I thought you would like a fire. I know I do." He began moving to the door, but I didn't move from the bath. "That would be someone to light it for us."

John opened the door and quietly chatted with the employee. Once the fire was lit, the person left and I exited the bath. Moving to the fire, I held out my hands. "It does feel good."

"Yes, it does." His hands came around me and he slowly pulled me close. "Sure you don't want to look around the place?"

Shaking my head, I felt him move from me.

"I'm going to take a shower then."

"Shower?" The heat felt good, but I turned to him. He was probably the cleanest person I ever saw.

John's hands came over his head and I saw him slip off his shirt. As he threw it to the bath floor, I felt my breath catch. The sight of my husband's toned body always surprised and excited me. He was the most handsome man I had ever seen. Leaning against the doorway, his midnight boots came off along with his dark socks. Turning to me, I saw him reach for his black belt with the shiny silver buckle. I swallowed the lump in my throat. Turning to the fireplace, I closed my eyes.

"Perhaps you should shut…" *Oh please don't!* "The bath door." *You don't really want him to do that! Yes, I do.* "For privacy. Your privacy." *Shut up! No!*

"It's just my wife and myself. I don't see why I need to be so modest."

He's right, you know. *No, he's not! Shut it!* "You're right." A part of me high-fived itself. Another part of me sulked. I frowned.

"We have no reason to be modest around one another, Phoenix. I love you exactly like you are and I know you love me. We should get used to seeing one another."

"I know that." Shaking my head, I concentrated on the flames.

The sound of the belt buckle being unlatched and being set down came to my ears. The zipper sound came next and the sound of John slipping off his jeans.

Closing my eyes and knowing it was a trick, I could feel John's presence reaching for me. Why could I feel him from so far away? And his scent! Oh my! Even from across the room, I could smell the scent that was uniquely John Westerling. Feeling myself sway, I caught myself and stood upright.

"Are you alright, Phoenix?"

Hearing footsteps come across the room, I held up a hand. The footsteps stopped. No way was I looking over to him! "I'm okay. Just a little lightheaded."

"Want to join me? The shower is big and could accommodate both of us."

I am sure it would! *Do it!* No! Ugh! "I think…." Clearing my throat, I tried speaking again. The thought of showering with John was too much! "I'm good. Really. The heat…" *from your body is intense,* "from the fire feels nice." Flinging out my hands, I turned my head to smile at him.

That was such a mistake! So many times I had seen John without a shirt on but the sight of him unclothed... Oh… I was right! John's body was cut and so solid!

My head came back to the fire. Sweat beaded on my forehead and it wasn't from the warmth of the fireplace. Resisting the urge to run from the suite or into John's arms, I dug in my heels to where I was standing. The feeling of being terribly afraid and overwhelmingly aware was confusing and uncomfortable. The magnetic draw my husband had could overwhelm my senses.

"You are always welcome to join me." With that, I heard him turn. There was no sound of the door shutting and I sighed loudly. At least he could shut the door so I didn't have to just turn and watch him bathe.

Just take one foot and pivot, a part of me urged myself. *You would be in full sight of your husband with the soap and water cascading down…*

"Thank you." Knowing I was too late, I said the words anyway.

"Did you say something?"

Shaking my head once, I closed my eyes and then opened them. "No!" Slapping my hand over my mouth, I sighed again. That was loud!

Maybe unpacking my things would calm my nerves. Unzipping my suitcase, I opened a dresser drawer and heard John moving around in the shower. Little noises and sounds. A moan or a hiss. What was he doing in there? Once again resisting the urge, I began emptying the few things from my case. As I did, I heard the water turn off. John's feet hit the floor and I tuned him out. Focus on the unpacking…

"Sorry."

Hearing John come up behind me now, I tensed and turned to him.

"I forgot my robe."

My eyes were glued to his body and I stared. I honestly think there are marble statues somewhere that looked exactly like his body. Chiseled and tight. Swallowing loudly, I stepped back and brought my hands behind my back. My hands smashed between my body and the dresser behind me. "Ouch."

"Are you okay?" Still naked, he came to me as I moved my hands around me. Taking my hands in his, he looked them over. At least I think he did. I couldn't take my eyes from his face. They weren't dropping any lower that was for sure. His individual kiss to them set off a spark inside me. "Looks fine."

His eyes held mine as he held my hands in his. *Yes, yes he did.* Feeling myself beginning to move toward him, I pulled my hands from his and stepped around him. Careful not to touch him, I moved to the bed. "It is fine."

John's lips turned up into a handsome smile.

What did I say? *It is fine.* "I mean, my hands." Bringing them up to show him, I realized what I did and dropped them. "You said…" Twisting my hands in front of me now, I looked to them. "You forgot your…" *what was that thing,* "robe. You forgot your robe."

Leaning down, I picked it up off the bed and walked over to him. Just within his reach of the robe, I held it out for him to take. I wasn't getting any closer to him than necessary.

"Thank you." His eyes held mine and I blushed.

"Don't you want it?" Looking to the robe, I held it out a little more.

"Of course I want it," his eyes glided slowly up and down my body, "but I am not going to take it."

"But I'm offering it to you." The robe shook in my hands, but his eyes never left mine.

"Are you, Phoenix?"

John's voice dropped into the sexiest timbre I had ever heard in my life and my mind went blank.

"Would you offer it to me without any cajoling or effort on my part? No tiptoeing around?" His step toward me wasn't menacing, but I felt my senses comes to high alert.

Of course I was offering him the robe! It was in my hand. "It's yours. Why wouldn't you take it?"

"Because love demands more of me. I can't just take it because it's mine now. I have to earn its trust as well as its love. It has to want me, too. Wanting it isn't enough."

"It's just a robe." Bringing it to me now, I saw his eyes move to where I clutched it against me.

"I'm not talking about the robe." His liquid grey eyes found mine and I saw his tongue come out for just a moment. "I'm talking about you."

"Me?" What had we been saying in the last few moments? I couldn't remember. Truthfully I didn't want to. "What about me?"

"You may be mine now and I may be yours, but I won't take you against your will. I won't have you because I can." His hands moved to his sides and he fisted them. "I want you to want me."

Gulping, I held the robe tighter to me. What was I supposed to say to that?! My complete focus was on John and I tried to fight it. I really did.

Slowly with one hand out he came to me. He didn't touch me. He really didn't have to. I could feel him from across the room. "You already want me." Fingertips lightly fell on my cheeks and caressed them. My eyes fell closed. "You already surrender to me. Can you feel it? My touch."

Not wanting to move my head, I stood still and just felt. His fingertips moved down my neck to my collarbone. I could feel their heat through my shirt.

"You're so beautiful. I still can't get over that you are mine." Tracing down my arms to my fingertips, I felt them move back up to my shoulder. The reverence in his voice was my undoing and the tear just behind my eyelid slid down my cheek. "You aren't afraid of me, are you?"

"No." Moving my head slightly, I opened my mouth. "I'm afraid of me." John moved flush with me and I caught my breath. "Because I would let you have me." My eyes opened and I looked into his. "I would let you ravish me like the Big Bad Wolf that you are."

He blinked but didn't move.

"You would be my undoing. I would let you do whatever you wanted with me and I wouldn't care as long as you loved me." Another tear traced down my cheek and I saw him look to it. "I want you. Don't ever doubt that."

"Then be with me, Little Red. Make love to me."

"Make love to you?" Blinking, I saw him move. His fingertips were still on my cheeks, but I was following him because he was right. I wanted to make love to him.

He sat on the bed and wrapped his arms around my waist. His head rested on my chest. "Use me, Phoenix. Tonight. Do anything you want with me."

John wanted me to use him? That's not how it worked. Was it?

"As much as you want to be with me, I want you. I don't care how you want to do this as long as we are together." Looking up at me, I saw his mouth turned down a little. His light beard and mustache looked wrong when he had a pleading face. My hand came to him and he leaned into it. John was surrendering himself to me.

"What if I can't? What if I am bad? What if I…"

"Am very good?"

I hated how his voice flowed over me so sensually. It crept into every part of my soul and made its home there.

"What if you are very good at it?" His hands came up to my face and he slanted it down to look at him. "What if you were the best lover I ever had? What if I didn't ever want to leave this bed because I knew you were the only woman to ever satisfy me? And I knew I would only ever feel at home was when I was with you?"

"You can't feel that way," I said, breathlessly.

John stood now and I looked up to my husband. "Why?"

"Because that's how I feel when I am with you." His hand came to me and I rested my cheek into it.

"Then we both know we have found something very special, my love. And we must hold onto it as tightly as we can." His other hand came to my cheek and righted my head. "I want to kiss you."

My heart beat wildly as I peered into his eyes.

"Can I kiss you, Little Red?"

Chapter 3 "Colour Me In" – Damien Rice

"You can, Big Bad."

His lips met mine in a light kiss that was more of an exploration. Drawing back just a little, I felt his lips meet mine and his mouth opened. The kiss was taking my breath away as I felt him take more of me into him. As he pulled me into his arms, I kissed him with everything I had. I wanted him to know that I loved him and that I was his. His kisses were expert and his mouth decadently divine. I could draw from him forever.

When his lips left mine I felt bereft.

"How do you want to do this? Just tell me."

The command and control in his voice was overwhelming. I blinked. I was in his arms standing next to the bed. My body was under his spell and it was ready. But I was not.

I wiggled and he sat me down on the floor. Going to the veranda door, I turned to him. "I want to." *Don't I?* "But I just don't know if I can… allow myself to be with you. And it's not you. It's me. Completely and totally me."

A muscle in his jaw ticked and he turned. Clearing his throat, I saw his shoulders slump, then just as fast, they picked back up. "I ordered the tray when I asked for someone to come light the fire. Why don't you make yourself comfortable?"

As I watched, he slid on the robe and moved over to the fireplace. His back was to me now as I saw him staring at the fireplace.

I had failed him. As sure as I stood there staring at my oh-so-patient husband I knew I had not done

what he wanted. But John wouldn't say anything.
He would gather his strength and come back to me.

"I think I will go take that shower."

"I'll let you know when they bring the food."
John's voice was quiet as he spoke. I hated to hear
the feeling of rejection I knew I put in it.

Picking up my own soft robe, I went to the bath
and shut the door. Slipping out of my own clothes, I
made my way over to the open shower. There were
no walls around it and a drain sat in the floor.
Turning on the shower, I adjusted the temperature
and stepped in. The water slid down my body.
John had brought in my shower items to the bath,
setting them on a shelf just under the shower head.
Taking my time, I touched each of them
individually. He took such good care of me. How
could I not do this one thing for him?

I knew why, of course. Because the idea of
being with a man, even John, frightened me beyond
words. My rational mind knew that John was not
Charles. But the possibility that John could hurt me
like Charles did was very real. In no time since John
and I had known each other had he ever hurt me.

Pure selfishness moved through me and the
thought of not being what John needed washed over
me. I was broken. Defective. And I was his wife.
There was no way I could ever be what he needed.
Bringing my hands to my eyes, I cried softly. John
deserved so much more than me. So much better
than who I was. And I couldn't be that. I couldn't
be what he needed and the thought hurt me more
than any pain I ever knew. Even the pain of
Charles' leather strap. Gratefully I would take those

Blossom

stings more than the thought of never being what John deserved.

The floor of the bath was warm and wet as I fell to it and brought my knees to my chest. I draped one hand around them and the other to my head. He would leave me. I would be someone from his past and never know his touch again. It frightened me to believe that.

"Phoenix?"

John was in the bath, but I couldn't bring myself to care.

"Phoenix?" His footsteps were close and I heard him beside me. He was just outside the shower. "What's wrong?"

"John?" Raising my head, I looked around but couldn't see anything to cover myself. "You shouldn't be…" The pain of not being good enough sliced through me. "I can't be what you…"

"Oh, my love." Bending down, he took my hands and I stood. "Have you washed?"

"I couldn't…"

His hands turned off the water and picked up a towel.

"You can't…" Bringing my hands behind my back, I tried to hide the scars that could never be hidden. "See… me…"

A soft towel was wrapped around my head securely. My soft robe was slipped onto my shoulders and I was lifted into John's arms. "You've been crying. I could hear you outside the bath. What's wrong?"

I wanted to remember his scent when I was cast off. Burying my face in it, I sobbed. "You deserve

27

what I can't give you. You need a warm, willing wife and I'm not her. My life is sad and scarred. You should have someone so much better than me."

"My Phoenix." John sat down on the bed with me in his lap. His hand came to the towel in my hair. "I love you. I love your scars and your life. You are everything I need. Absolutely everything."

"I can't have sex with you. I can't make myself want to be with you in the physical way you want to be. I've never been with someone who is gentle. They have always used me. In pain and hurting, they would leave me and I would be alone to heal without them."

"Is that what you think of me?" His hand came to my cheek as he looked into my eyes. "That I would hurt you and leave you to take care of yourself without me after we make love?"

Adamantly I shook my head. I knew that wasn't John. It never would be.

"The tray arrived when you were in the shower. I set it by the fireplace. Why don't we rest there for a while and have some food. It's been a long day, has it not?"

"Yes." I let go of John's neck and tried to move from his lap.

"I like you there just fine." Standing with me in his arms, hands wrapped back around his neck, he brought us to the fireplace and sat. "Can you feel the warmth?"

"Yes." John felt so right. His dips fit perfectly into my curves. The warmth from his body was surrounding me again.

He took my hands into his and lowered his head. As I watched, he prayed for the food and for our safety. He asked that we have a good night and finished with an "Amen."

The small meal was a welcome repast. I didn't realize how hungry I was until I began eating. John ate his fair share, too, and soon the tray was empty.

"Feel a little more sated?"

"Yes." Standing up from his lap, I moved to the window and looked outside. I could see the shadow of lights. We were secluded in our own little paradise.

John moved over to the window with me. "It's so peaceful here, isn't it?"

"Uh-huh. You made an excellent choice."

We stood there for a few more minutes just looking out the window. It was quiet in the suite and I could hear John's breathing.

As he turned to me, I felt his eyes on me. "Would you like to do anything? Go out? Look around?"

"No. I like it here."

"I'm going to brush my teeth, then." Turning on his heel, he went to the bath. Little noises: the tear of floss, the scrape of the toothbrush, the gargle of mouthwash. John finished up in the bath and came back out. "I didn't know what you needed, but I set out your things like mine."

"Thank you." I didn't turn from the window.

"You're welcome." Hearing him sit, I turned and watched him.

"Why don't you come to the bed after you brush? I would just like to talk with you."

29

One last glance out the window and I went to the bath. John had set almost everything out for me. I used them, then made my way back to the bed and sat down on the other side of him.

John leaned back against the tall headboard and crossed his ankles. "It really is a wonderful facility. There is an onsite fitness facility that I would like to take advantage of in the morning. Might give you time to look around unless you would like to come with me."

I slipped into the same position on the other side of the bed. The idea of leaving the room without John terrified me, but I wouldn't tell him that.

"I'll be gone a few hours then we can explore what you find together. There are so many places to visit and see that I think you would like."

A yawn came to me as I lay down and turned to face John. His head slanted down to me, the gorgeous smile back on his face. I wanted to touch that smile. Instead I placed my hands under my chin. "Tell me about Anna."

"Anna." His eyebrows veed and he looked to his feet. They were wiggling on the bed. "She's the most beautiful girl I ever saw. When I first saw her I knew she was my heart and that I would do everything I could to protect her. I brought her home and cared for her." Looking to me, he smiled wider. "Two brothers. I didn't have a clue on how to take care of a little girl."

John had two brothers. I had met them at the reception. David and Jonathon. The introduction I had to them was at a point that I was beginning to feel overwhelmed with people. But I remembered them.

Jonathon was the younger. Honey-colored hair and brown eyes. He wore leather and smelled of gasoline. Rougher around the exterior than John. He was nice in the 'loner guy doing his own thing' way.

David was a card, always laughing. Long black hair and a welcoming face. John told me he was single, but I noticed David's eye kept wandering to a woman who had recently joined John's church. Evelyn Miller. Evelyn just came out of a divorce with a baby and toddler. My heart went out to her and I had spoken to her a few times. She seemed very nice but stressed. I liked her.

John laughed and I smiled at the sound, coming out of my musings. "I learned fast and she became my world. Going back to work for me was hard. I went through a few babysitters before Missy applied for the position."

"Missy LaFevre?" She was Anna's Sunday school teacher at their church.

"Yes. I wasn't sure about her at first. But when she held Anna, my daughter quieted and was fascinated by her. If she was good enough for Anna, she was good enough for me. Missy started the next day and has been taking care of Anna since."

"How old was Anna?"

"About six months." He folded his hands. "It was Missy that invited us to church. I didn't want to go, but Missy offered to take Anna and give me a few hours to myself. She was about two then.

Finding that I couldn't bear to be apart from my daughter and seeing Anna so happy, I started going, too. Soon after that I gave my life to the Lord and started walking the straight and narrow."

"You sound so religious. John Westerling, man of God!" I giggled and John half-heartedly laughed.

"Yeah. But I was so lost, Phoenix. One woman after another and no consistency in my life for Anna. I came home at the same time and spent every moment with her, but I needed more than her. I found that at our church."

One woman after another. I could see that. John was an exceptionally handsome man with the muscles and charisma to charm any woman. "I bet a lot of women chased you."

"There were some." He shrugged and smiled at me. "But they are nothing compared to my wife and our new life. I will always be faithful to her and our family."

I nodded my head and closed my eyes. "Your wife and family sound very lucky."

"I am a very blessed man." John took a breath and exhaled. "Phoenix?"

John's tone took on a serious note and I opened my eyes. He was going to say something important and I wanted to be completely attentive to him.

"Tonight I would like for us to sleep under the covers. Without our robes on."

The thought to run came to me, but I kept myself still.

"If you want to stay on that side, it's alright and I understand. But you are more than welcome to join me over here." His eyes narrowed and I saw the glittering grey jewels in the light. "I won't touch you unless you ask. And I certainly won't take advantage of your trust."

Swallowing, I watched him.

"Would you do that for me, Phoenix?"

Could I do that for him? Any other time we had slept together he was on top of the covers dressed for bed while I was dressed and underneath the covers. Taking a breath I held it and nodded. "Yes."

A big, handsome smile graced his mouth and he settled down on the bed with his head on the pillow. Turning his head to me, he smiled wider. "I love you."

"I love you, too."

We talked for a little while longer.

His childhood came from his lips to my ears. Laughter and tears. His mother and father were still living. I knew that, too, as I was introduced to them at the reception, too, but for some reason that hadn't stuck. His brothers were unmarried and David was a Deacon, whatever that was, at his church. I hadn't remembered meeting him the couple of times I had gone to John's church. He told me David often worked on Sundays and came when he was not scheduled. Jonathon was the wild one who didn't need God. He went all over the country on his bike, romancing one woman after another, moving on to the next thing. John and David were the responsible ones.

I told John about my growing up years, too. My older brother Harry and my father were always getting into trouble. My mother would always bail them out. My father was an alcoholic and by the

time Harry was fifteen, he was, too. When I married
Charles my dad was already out of my life. My
mother's death and Charles' denial of my family
sent Harry off, too. No other family, so with Charles
as my legal husband and the promise I made to him,
I stayed in the emotionally and physically abusive
marriage. That was until the day Charles died.
When that happened I could finally move on. John
and I were already friends and that friendship
developed into so much more.

By the end of our conversation we both knew
more about one another. I saw him sit up and untie
his robe. Slipping it from his shoulders, he shed it
and laid it across the end of our bed. Seeing him
that way still took my breath from me. He was more
than I could ever ask for.

A sigh escaped my lips. I sat up and untied my
belt. Turning from him, I took the robe off and slid
under the covers. I placed my robe on the other side
of the foot of the bed from John's. The covers were
up to my chin when I lay down.

"It's alright, Phoenix. I don't plan on coming
over there. You can relax."

I was relaxed, wasn't I? No, no, I wasn't. Every
muscle in my body felt tight. Consciously I made
the choice to slowly relax. Once they did, I breathed
a sigh of relief. The feather down bed felt luxurious
and I sank into it a little.

"I love you."

"I love you, too."

Quiet reigned in the room and I could hear
John's breathing. Although the room was
comfortable, I felt cold. Moving over just a little, I

watched him. His breathing didn't change. Once more I moved and could just barely feel John's body heat. One more move had me almost to him. His scent came next with more heat. Last move and I felt his body next to mine. I couldn't get over how right it felt to be next to him. Laying my head on his shoulder, he didn't move and I breathed a sigh of relief. Trying to find a comfortable spot for my head, I continued trying different spots on his shoulder.

"John? Can I ask...? Could you put your arm around my neck? I can't find a place to lay my head."

His arm moved up over my head, sliding under my neck. He didn't turn or move toward me. Resting my head on the spot between his shoulder and chest, still hard but softer than his shoulder, I sighed. His hand came to my waist but lay down on the bed.

For a few minutes I lay there appreciating the feel of being in John's arms. Sort of. Taking a chance, I curled into his side. John's breathing changed just a little, but I held my place. My curves fit into him again. His hand moved to my shoulder, but he didn't move.

Looking at him in the almost dark, I just knew what I wanted. It was what he wanted, too. "John?"

"Yes?"

"I want to... make love... to you."

He didn't move but remained perfectly still. "Are you sure?"

I lifted my head and cupped his face. His cheek was warm as I pressed my lips against it. "Yes. Just don't…" I bit my lip, "please, don't hurt me."

John turned in to me now and I took my hand from him. His came to my cheek and his thumb caressed my lip. "I would never hurt you, Little Red. Do you believe that?"

My body was already softening toward his and I nodded my head. "Yes." And I did. "I do. Big Bad."

"Then make love to me."

I watched him for a moment. John was so different from any other man I ever knew. Everything he had ever done made that abundantly clear. I realized then that I wanted to be with him. That I would throw caution to the wind and make love to my husband.

The kiss to him was consuming. I gave him everything I had never given any other man. My heart, my soul, and my life. It was all his now.

That was the last thought I had as my arms slid around his neck and he gently pulled me to him.

Chapter 4 "This Place Is A Shelter" - Olafur Arnalds

When I was married to my first husband, the few times he would come to my room and have nonconsensual sex with me, I couldn't stay on the bed. The thought of lying in the same spot as where I was brought so much pain and degradation it was humiliating and shameful. So I had taken to sleeping on the floor after the attacks. Even now after making such achingly sweet love to my husband I couldn't make myself stay on the bed with him. Those memories of Charles were too rooted in me to change so quickly.

My head was resting on John's chest and I could feel his breathing evenly. He was fast asleep, but I had lain here on him for a while now wide awake. Even in my exhaustion I couldn't sleep. Not on the bed.

I pulled the comforter off the bed and wrapped myself in it. I pulled the sheet to cover John's exquisite body and sighed. It should never be covered. The carpet didn't make a sound as I moved to the corner and sat, huddling in the darkness.

It wasn't John that drew me from the bed. If anything he would be the one keeping me there. The magnetism I felt to him was strong.

The care and consideration John showed me during the entire time we were together was beyond anything I had ever known with another man. Next to John's tender concern there had never been another man in my life. Only selfish lovers.

A tear slid down my cheek as I remembered how he had taken his time with me, making sure I was completely satisfied before he even began to ask for himself. His patience with me seemed infinite and for that I was grateful. From the moment we began to make love, so slow and sensual, he had never taken from me but only gave. His touches were light and soothing, his presence calming and sure. When I had finally initiated the act itself, John was so encouraging and patient with me. He told me he wanted me to be satisfied again before he gave in to his desires with me. When I finally did, he came undone and we were both lost to the pleasures that only we could give to one another.

My body so alive after being so intimate with my husband, and that being a new experience, I couldn't help but contrast John with Charles. John gave. Charles took. John's touches were light, almost like air passing over my skin. Charles was pinching and cruel. John made sure I was completely ready. Charles took me without a thought. John held me after our time together was over. Charles rolled off of me and left the room. John was calm and serene. Charles had been chaotic and disastrous.

"Phoenix?"

John's voice drew me out of my musings and I pulled the comforter tighter to myself. Would he understand why I was sitting in the corner wrapped in a comforter trying to change my patterns but finding I couldn't?

He sat up and looked around the room. In the dim light, I saw him find me. "What are you doing on the floor, my love?"

Trying to speak but not finding myself able to, I shook my head.

His hand came out and I saw his fingers wiggle. "Come back to bed."

It was an invitation to lie down. I knew that. Nothing more. He sounded tired, of which I had no doubt. But as exhausted from our cravings as I was, I knew John was more resilient.

He slid off the bed and padded over to me. I was never more grateful for the cover of night as I was now. His body was in shadow but still so masculine. As he bent down in front me, I saw him clasp his hands. "What are you thinking?"

The lump was hard in my throat as I swallowed it. I shook my head, knowing I couldn't speak right now.

"Okay." Standing, he made his way back to the bed and slid on his robe. Making his way back over to me, he sat down in the floor. "Phoenix? Will you tell me why you are sitting on the floor? In the corner of the bedroom?"

My head came up and down once.

"Can I hold your hand?"

Nodding my head again, I brought one hand out of the comforter and grasped his.

"Your hand is so cold." Sliding over to me, he put an arm around me. "We're in this together and we've promised that we would talk this out."

I nodded my head. "When I was married to Charles… after he would come to my room at night to…"

"Yes." The steel was back in his voice.

"I couldn't stay on the bed after… it. In the shower I would scrub my body until I was almost bleeding, but I still couldn't get him off of me. When I was finally so tired of fighting myself, I would take my blanket and wrap up in the corner of the room. I couldn't do it, be on the bed afterwards. Not when I knew that was the one place that I was in so much pain in." Bringing my hands to my eyes, I cried.

John turned to me and took me in his arms. Whispering soothing little words to me, he rocked me slowly. When I had finally calmed down, he took my face carefully in his hands and I looked up to him. "Is that how you feel when you are with me? Now that we have made love?"

My head adamantly shook. "No! What we did was nothing like what happened to me with Charles!" Sitting up in front of him now, the comforter wrapped around my shoulders, I took his hands. "You are and have always been the exact opposite of his selfishness. You are love and light. Joy and peace. Everything he never was!"

"Then why are you on the floor?" His white teeth stood out against the night. "Why won't you come back to the bed?"

My eyes found the bed now. I know it was me, but it looked so imposing, so ominous. "I didn't shower when I left the bed. Your scent is all over me, in me. I can feel you all around me, especially…" I blushed knowing exactly where I still felt him even though he wasn't there anymore. "I've never felt this way before, never done what I have done with you tonight, with another man. No man has ever brought me the pleasure you have."

His chuckle was righteous and knowing. He knew what I was saying was true. Eyes narrowing at me now, he took my by the shoulders. His face came close to my ear and I could hear him breathing. "I would make love to you again. Kiss you until you couldn't think about anything except the feel my lips on your skin, my fingers on your beautiful body. You were made to love me and I was made to be loved by you."

Yes! No! Yes! Wait! My eyes found his again. "I want that more than anything in the world."

"We're married, Phoenix. We can do anything we want with one another. I will only ever touch you in love and your touch to me is…" John faltered now. "Is more exhilarating than anything I have ever known."

Heat rose in my cheeks. The memories of the consummation of our marriage was the best memory I would ever have of us.

"Come to bed." Standing, he looked down to me and held out a hand.

The bed caught my attention again and I looked back to my husband. "I can't."

"Well, then," his hands came under me, lifting me from the floor, "I think it is time you learn that sometimes I know what's best."

His tone was teasing and I wasn't frightened. I knew he was trying to help me overcome my fear, but I was stubborn. "What are you doing?!"

"Taking my wife to bed. This is my honeymoon, too." He sat me down on the bed and slipped off his robe. Lying back down, his arm wrapped around my waist, he pulled me to him. The surprise movement caused me to topple backwards onto the bed. He caught me and held me in his arms. "If you want to stay wrapped up in the blanket, by all means do so. But on my honeymoon night, I will lie next to my wife on the bed in which I made love to her."

"John Westerling!" Trying to move from him, I brought myself against him more securely. "Let me go!"

"Phoenix Westerling! I will not!" His mouth covered mine in a hard kiss that took my breath away.

I fought him. Oh, I fought him. Because he was right and because my life with John was not my life with Charles. My whole idea of what I had done for the last five years was shifting and I was becoming a different person.

The kiss changed into a softer, more cajoling one. I could feel my resolve slip away. My arms went around his neck as my mouth welcomed his tongue into it. My body had a mind of its own as it pressed against John's. He pulled away from me and I grunted.

"What do you want, Phoenix?"

"Please..." Not really sure if it was to get off the bed or stay in my husband's arms, I looked to him.

"I made a promise to you and my daughter. And I intend to do everything I can to see it fulfilled!"

His lips found me again as he slid the comforter from my body and I surrendered to his masterful touches.

***

From the Journal of John Westerling
November 21st
The Day After Our Wedding Day

The inn has been very accommodating to Phoenix and me. I picked it for Phoenix as much as myself. I wanted some place I could feel at peace to help Phoenix. She needed some place to begin her healing. This was the perfect spot for our new lives as a couple to begin.

I wanted to wake up this morning to my wife in my arms. To feel her wrapped around me maybe with her hand on my chest. Her hair somewhere tangled in my body. Maybe her toes jabbing into my calves. Her smile to me as I woke her with a kiss would have been the best way to start the morning.

Instead Phoenix is back on the floor where I found her last night. She must have slipped out of bed when I fell asleep again this morning. Wrapped in the comforter tightly around her like a shield. I know now why, but I still don't have to like it. I know she's not afraid of me but of the memories even our lovemaking creates in her. Having done my best to try to keep her on the bed last night even to the point of feeling the aches myself, my wife has made her way off the bed and back to where I found her on the floor.

Phoenix was right when she calls Charles selfish. Any man who treats a woman like he treated her deserves to be castrated and tied to a post for the buzzards to pick at his still-warm flesh.

This may take time for her to break this habit—as I am sure it is a habit—with her. I just have to be patient and love her.

We have the whole day to ourselves. It is a honeymoon that I will always cherish. I love my wife so much and I want this to be so good for her. Breakfast after the shower this morning and then I need to be off to the fitness center. I'll ask Phoenix if she wants to go with me, but I am never really sure what she is thinking. I hope my guesses have been spot-on. I pray to be the husband she needs and wants, but I am not really sure.

Sometimes when she looks at me I think she isn't really seeing me but Charles. I am nothing like him, I could never be, but his ghost still lives on in her. I am trying, but one day I hope to have her see me, John, her now husband.

Only God can cause this to happen. This is my prayer…

***

The kiss on my lips surprised me. I could taste John on them and it comforted me. The sigh that escaped them was cleansing. My John.

He was sitting in front of me and a fleeting thought that I should make breakfast or clean the house came to me. But we were at an inn and breakfast would be downstairs already cooked. Did he want me to do something for him? Now that we were married had the rules changed and were there certain expectations I was supposed to know or meet for him?

His smile was killer. Dark skin, white teeth. That mouth could bring so much pleasure. I would never look at it the same way again.

"Good morning."

The voice of my husband moved across my soul again and embraced me. I could listen to him all day and never tire of hearing him speak. I smiled, licking my lips, wanting his taste in me. "Good morning."

"I see you are back." His eyes looked around me and then came back to mine.

"Yeah." Tears threatened, but I wouldn't let them fall. He knew now, why I was here. Was he angry? Upset that I had failed him?

"My Phoenix." Crouching on the floor in front of me, he reached for my hands. "Pray with me so that we may begin our day."

Clasping his hands, I smiled. When our hands touched I felt a peace course through my soul. My eyes moved from our joined hands to his eyes. Did he feel that, too?

John's head bent and his eyes closed. "Dear Heavenly Father, we come to You today as one praising Your name. We thank You for this new life you have given us together. May our marriage be used for Your glory and honor. May we always walk in Your way united as one. We thank You for this day You have given us. Help us to have a good one. In Your name I pray. Amen."

"Amen." Repeating John's last words was almost unconscious. A part of me accepted his faith now and needed the sameness of his routine. Lifting my eyes to his, I smiled. "I should be very mad at you."

"For what?" Taking my hands, he brought me upright to him.

"Picking me up like a child and taking me to bed."

"Like this?" He swept me up in his arms, and I hit his chest playfully. He was so solid.

"Yes, like that." My arms looped around his neck and I rested my head on his shoulder. There was no place in the world I would rather be.

"Are you mad about what happened on the bed when I…"

"No!" I blushed as we moved to the bath. Sitting me down, he slid the comforter from my body and dropped it to the floor. "I just think…"

"You think too much." His kiss was swift and demanding. Hands found my shoulders and pulled me to it. John Westerling was a master with his entire body and he knew how to gently dominate mine. I could feel myself giving over to him as he plundered me.

When he broke the kiss and cleared his throat, I saw him turn from me to start the shower.

Holy smokes! What was that?

My hand went to the sink and I steadied myself. I was ready to give myself up to him right now and John acted as if nothing happened.

He stepped into the shower and held out his hand. "Join me."

Blossom

How could a man have the body and mind of an angel and the voice and magnetism of a devil? Almost without thought I felt myself moving toward him. Clasping his hand, I stepped in.

A washcloth and my soap were placed in my hand and I began washing. I had never showered with anyone before and this intimate act with my husband made this new experience that much more profound.

My glances kept coming back to him as I washed. His powerful hands were mesmerizing as he moved them through his long, dark hair. The arch of his back as his strong hands came through to rinse out the shampoo. The slant of his mouth so concentrated on the task. The smell of his soap as he lathered his muscular body and then used the water to rinse it off. The scrape of the razor without a mirror as he shaved around his mustache and light beard so precisely. I wanted to ask how he knew how to do that without seeing what he was doing, but he looked so practiced and I really didn't want to know. It was part of the magic that was my husband.

"Are you finished?" John was looking over his shoulder toward me as he watched me.

My head bobbed up and down once. Speaking when he was watching me so intensely was completely impossible. Especially since we were both naked in the shower.

He turned off the water and stepped out, handing me a towel.

Did he not feel the same attraction to me that I did to him? Had his ardor cooled now that we had

47

made love twice? The entire time we had showered he hadn't faced me and even now he wasn't.

The towel was already around his waist and he was standing still.

Wrapping the towel around my own body, I stepped out. John was unusually quiet.

"Is something wrong?"

His hands fisted at his sides but he didn't turn.

"Did I do something..?"

John turned then and faced me. I was taken away at his sheer masculinity as it came to me. "I am trying to restrain myself."

"From what?" The idea to back up against the shower because of the raw power emanating from my husband came to me, but I stood my ground.

"From laying you on the bed again and having my way with you."

"Oh." I blinked a couple of times and felt my heart race. Swallowing, I stood very still, trapped under his narrowing gaze.

His arm muscles flexed and bulged as he flexed his hands. "But we can't spend all day here in this room on the bed. Can we, Phoenix?"

Was that a question? Was he asking my permission?

Stalking up to me, he took me gently by the shoulders. "No matter how much I like... eating cheesecake with you, we can't stay in the room, can we?"

My head shook back and forth. Was that the answer he was looking for? Because I really wanted to say yes.

Chapter 5 "Chances" – Five for Fighting

"I didn't think so." His shoulders slumped and then picked back up. One hand came out and captured mine. "Let's dress then." The smile was back in his voice. "Breakfast is a buffet and I don't know about you, but I am starving. Afterwards, if you like, you could come with me to the fitness center."

His hand left mine and he began to dress. I picked out my own clothes, too, and began dressing with my back to John. I tried to keep my hair over the scars on my back, but I knew I couldn't the whole time. John's glances were tangible as I heard him continuing to dress. My body seemed to gravitate toward his like some sort of field he emanated to draw me in. But I resisted the urge and began thinking of something else. The idea of going with John was intriguing and as great at that sounded, I really wanted some time to myself.

"I think I want to stay here. Collect myself. Check things out." *Not leave the room if I don't have to.* "We could explore together when you are done."

"Sounds like a great idea!" John's feet moved now and I turned to see him dressed. The scrape of the toothbrush and a few other small noises. When he emerged, he looked absolutely perfect. His shirt was an off-white Henley with its only two buttons undone. Over that was a jet-black wool pea coat with its collar standing up. Dark washed denim jeans with his belt and modest silver buckle. His buckled midnight boots encapsulated his feet. His presence was reaching for me as his eyes took me in.

I was dressed now, too. A light grey soft wool sweater with its mock neck and long sleeves accompanied my light denim jeans. Grey boots with fur grazed the top of my ankles and fit over my jeans. My hair was brushed and still damp down around my shoulders to finish drying.

John came to me and took me in his arms. His smile was wide as he looked down to me. I couldn't understand why he did that. Watched me like he did. It was as if he were ready to attack anything that stood between him and myself. Maybe that's what it was. "What?"

"I was just thinking. You have holes in your ears."

The tiny silver hoops that hung in each of his earlobes shone in the light. "So do you."

"But I wear my earrings. You don't. Why?" He sounded genuinely intrigued.

"I don't have any jewelry." My lips lifted and I tried to move out of his arms. He wouldn't let me go.

"No jewelry?"

"No. Except for…" I felt my engagement ring and wedding band. The band was a thinner representation of John's wider one. "If that's the only pieces I ever have I am more than content."

"Did you not have any jewelry you wanted to bring from your house?"

"I didn't…" Clearing my throat, I glanced at him, then his Adam's apple. It bobbed. "Charles never bought me anything and I really didn't need it." My lips lifted again then fell. "It's alright."

His arms slipped from around my waist. Going to his suitcase, he lifted out a box and brought it over to me.

"What is that?"

"A wedding gift. Open it."

"But I didn't get you anything."

"You gave me you." He pressed the box into my hand. "I know what it took for you last night. To give yourself to me. Your gift was the best thing you could ever give me."

A tear fell down my cheek as I remembered our wedding night. It was the most beautiful experience I had ever known. "I love you. How could I not?"

His laughter reverberated through the room. "To hear you say that is music, Phoenix. And I will take it as often as I can. But I know you could have chosen not to ask me to let you make love to me. I know you could have stayed on the other side of the bed. Last night could have gone so many different ways but to me," he stroked my hair with his hand, "it was everything I could have ever asked for because you are everything I need."

The box was silver with a shiny red bow wrapped around it. Sliding the bow off, I opened the box. The gasp was involuntary as I beheld two tiny ruby heart earrings with a matching silver chained necklace with a matching ruby. Each of the rubies had little diamonds surrounding them. "John."

"You are my Little Red. I wanted to give you something to match my name for you." His hand came out. "May I?"

I couldn't tear my eyes from the beauty that the box contained. The rubies and diamonds were magnificent, but what was more magical to me was that John had gotten them for me. He had bought me a gift.

The ruby-and-diamond studs were so miniscule in his hands, but he held them so delicately. He took his time sliding each one into my ears and clasping them. His touch almost nonexistent. I could hear him barely breathing as he touched my shoulder and I turned. The necklace lay on my chest and looking down, I could see it twinkle in the sunlight. They were such delicate pieces of jewelry.

My arms came around my husband and kissed him. I tried hard to pour all the love and hope and care I felt for him into that kiss. The memory of it, of how I felt right now, wanted to sear itself onto my brain.

John's arms slid around my waist and pulled me close. His nudge had me jumping to wrap my legs around his waist as he deepened the kiss. I could feel us moving, but I didn't care. In my husband's most capable arms, I would allow him take me anywhere.

His hands stayed on my waist, to my frustration. My hands slid into his hair, freeing it from the restriction of the ring that held it back. The hair slid forward and covered our faces. I loved to feel my husband's hair on my cheeks.

Breaking the kiss, John panted. "We can't stay here today." His mouth dove for mine and I sighed into it.

Why? Why couldn't we stay here? Or was he asking me again? Seeking my permission? Did it really matter? But yes, it did matter. I knew John had planned to go to the fitness center and I was starving. Last night's endeavors had depleted the light meal we had eaten and I barely ate anything the day of our wedding. Pulling back from him, I gulped in a big breath of air. "Breakfast!"

His look to me was quizzical as if he had no clue what I was talking about. Slowly his face changed and I could see the resignation in it. He wasn't happy, but I knew he had made the decision.

Secretly I was good either way.

He stood and took my hands, pulling me to my feet. His arms slid around my waist, pulling me to his side. "You are right, wife. I am hungry."

Knowing for what, I held my tongue. He wasn't talking about food and we both knew it.

The buffet downstairs was huge, a lot of it made to order. I chose an assortment of food that I knew I wouldn't have at John's house.

Our house. I had to remember it was our home, not just his. Wasn't it? As I filled my already too-full plate, I remembered Charles had always called the house his. Not ours. Even though he had left it to me in his will, it was still his. Putting it on the market was one of the best decisions I had ever made. The house would go to new owners. People who would fill it with love and happiness. We never had that, Charles and I. Constant mental and physical abuse abounded in that house, but the new owners would never know that. They would never know how many times I had to clean my own blood off of the floor after Charles had taken that leather lash to me and my back. How hard it was to get the blood off the carpet and wood floors. How many times Charles had come to my room to hurt me in the night.

"Phoenix?"

I blinked and saw John sitting across from me at a small table. The table was solid but wavered in my vision as I looked to it through misty eyes. John was looking at me nervously.

"You're as white as a sheet."

Shaking my head, I tried to smile and took his hand. When John prayed, the ghosts that haunted me retreated and I knew peace. It was an odd feeling, not being religious as John was. His Christianity was somehow a healing balm to my soul. I wasn't sure how, but when he spoke to his God, it brought me comfort. "Pray for our meal." *For me.* My head bowed and I waited. When John wasn't forthcoming, I looked up. He was bowing his head now with his eyes closed. His fingers threaded through mine and he squeezed them.

"Dear Heavenly Father, maker of heaven and earth. I pray today for my wife. I pray that You bring her comfort and strength. I pray that You show her Your love. Help me to show her Your love. Help me to be everything she needs here on earth. Thank You for Anna and be with her, Missy, and Dale. Help them to have a good day as well. Thank You for this food and for Your love to us. Amen."

"Amen." I squeezed his fingers now as I felt him beginning to let go of mine. My eyes found his and I smiled. The ghosts had retreated as he had prayed and once again I felt love wrap itself around my heart. "Thank you."

"You're welcome."

When he leaned forward, I did, too, and we kissed. It was a light, lingering kiss that that brought me reassurance. When I went to pull my hand out of his, he lifted it to his lips and kissed it. Placing it gently on the table, he let my hand go. Immediately I missed his touch.

"The inn has many activities going on during the day. Most of which you could just show up for. There is a brochure back in our room. If you want, I could look over them with you when we get back." John began eating rather heartily. Bacon, sausage, eggs—things I knew he didn't keep at home. At least I had never seen there. Fresh fruit was in a bowl beside his plate, but it was the heavier foods I saw him eat.

"I think I got it." The self-assurance in my voice surprised me. John stopped chewing for a moment, looked to me, smiled, and then went back to his food. "Besides," I cleared my throat, "you have other things you need to do and I wouldn't ever want to keep you from them. I'm fine, really."

We finished eating with much gusto, drinking our coffee and chatting quietly about the inn. Soon, he took my hand and we made our way back up to the room. John pulled his workout clothes out of the suitcase and I looked to them.

"Where are your workout shorts?"

"Workout…?"

"The ones you wear at your home that are too tight and very…" My eyes widened as I covered my mouth. Gulping, I heard him laugh. His smile was easy and his laugh deep. Had I not been the same color as the rubies adorning my ears and throat, I would have felt compelled to laugh, too. I took my hand off of my mouth. "The black ones…" I stuttered. "The ones that…" Indicating his waist, I sighed dramatically as his laughter increased. "Forget it." Pivoting on one foot, I felt my waist caught and I was brought up to him.

"The too-tight shorts are compression shorts." He snickered softly in my ear and I shivered. "I didn't realize they were too tight."

"Of course they are!" Any sane person could see… nothing left to the imagination when he wore them! How could he not see that?

"I didn't realize you were looking at them." Turning me in his arms, he watched my eyes.

"How could I not?" Wait! Did I just admit that I was watching him with them on? His slow and easy smile told I had.

"I mean…" Moving out of his arms, I began tidying the room unnecessarily. "They are probably, maybe, beneficial to your workout and I thought that you…" He was standing behind me now. The expression on his face was one of complete seriousness as he looked me over.

"The compression shorts do maximize my workout. And I am glad my *wife* admires them on me. I'll have to remember that when we get home."

His presence reached for me again. It felt like in the horror movies when an unseen hand pulled a

person toward their fate. That person was usually
kicking and screaming, but I knew I wouldn't. Like
a sheep to the slaughter, I would follow John
anywhere he led.

"I just meant…"

The hands on my face were lightning quick and
his touch caressing. His eyes found my lips. "You
desire your husband."

"You weren't my husband then."

His hands took mine and he leaned his forehead
against mine. "When I proposed to you on your
front porch, even though you said you had to think
about it, I was already married to you in my heart.
When you came over and found me downstairs in
my too-tight shorts," his light laugh made me smile,
"it was because I had already betrothed myself to
you. No other woman has or will ever see me in
them except you. So yes, my love," the kiss to my
forehead curled my toes, "I was already your
husband." He let go of me and began changing.
"Just not legally married to you in the eyes of the
law."

His hands picked up a t-shirt with three-
quarter-length sleeves almost the same color as the
rubies and also a pair of black knit pants.

I really should look away from him, I thought
as he slipped off his clothes piece by piece and laid
them on the bed. Not watch him as he pulled off his
shirt or jeans to replace them with loose-fitting knit
versions of the same clothing. Black athletic shoes
replaced his boots and he tied back his almost coal-
black hair. I should have but didn't. He was mine

now and I could watch him. He said I could. And I wanted to! "And what if I had said no?"

"I knew you. You wouldn't have." His grey eyes searched mine and I knew he was right. As committed as he was then to me, I was also his. I may not have admitted it at the time, but anytime I needed a friend he was always there. John Westerling knew me too well.

"So your workout?" Desperately needing to change the subject, I moved from his arms to the door. "How long will you be doing that today?"

Striding over, he took my hand and opened the door. "Last night was a good all-around routine." A couple walked by in the hall as John talked. They glanced knowingly to us as they passed.

"John!" Blushing, I watched them enter the elevator. He was already pulling me to it, but I didn't want to ride the same one as the couple who just heard John admit that we had made love.

"Phoenix!" We made the elevator anyway and I stepped partially behind John. Not only out of trepidation but out of embarrassment.

"A few hours then. I really want to push myself for our next sessions this evening. I want to be ready to take you whenever and wherever I can."

I heard the couple laugh quietly.

"Really?" He glanced to me as he held my hand. The almost-ever-present smile was back on his face.

"Yes, really. I never know what you want and I have to be ready to do it at a moment's notice." He sounded so sincere, but I couldn't help but blush redder.

"Seriously?"

"Yes. There are a lot of historical landmarks around here and restaurants of which you get to pick this evening where to dine. Attentiveness to my love is key to our marriage. And I plan to be the most attentive husband… to all of your needs."

The couple laughed outright and I slapped his shoulder playfully. Thankfully the elevator doors opened and the couple laughed as they walked down the opposite hall from us. John still had my hand in his, walking without a care in the world. "Do you have to announce our love life to everyone?"

"Everyone? It was just a guy and girl. Married, by the way. Matching wedding bands." He held his up and looked to mine. "I would say I inspired them." Moving close to me, he smiled conspiratorially. "Although I stopped talking about our love life after I stepped out of the suite's door."

My mouth dropped open! He had been talking about an outing and dinner that way? My husband was good! "I can't believe you did that."

The door to the fitness room was in front of us now and I could hear the music. It was loud. There were already several people inside lifting weights, walking on the treadmills, doing various routines. Too many people for me. "Looks like I am here." The kiss on my cheek was chaste and warm. "Sure you don't want to stay?"

"No." Unfamiliarity, the loud music, and the abundance of people turned me off of it. Turning, I waved my hand. "Have fun."

"I love you." The music got louder and I turned to see the door open. John's eyes were lit up like Christmas.

"I love you, too."

He stepped inside and began greeting people. I watched him for a bit, moving around the room. Warm smile, offering a hand of greeting. My husband was a very open individual and I realized as I watched him that I envied that in him. His willingness to put himself out there. To be critiqued and become fast friends with strangers. In a way I wanted to be able to do that, too. But I wasn't sure if I ever could. Not the way John did.

Turning again, I made my way down the hall and found a booklet about the inn. Where to start poking around?

Chapter 6 "Just Give Me a Reason" – P!nk

The swimming pool area was immense, with a hot tub and sauna room. A sky view from the floor looked out over the town. A yoga session ran just about every hour for anyone who wanted to participate. Trails outside the hotel offered guests the chance to walk nature trails of varied outdoor scenes. But it was the boutique that caught my eye.

As I moved around the brightly-lit room an idea came to me. I doubted they would have what I wanted, but I would look anyway. The greeting I had when I came to the door was warm and I was told if I needed anything to ask. A blush stained my cheeks as I thought of what I wanted.

"Are you finding everything, Miss?"

The same woman who greeted me came back to me now. She was tall with a graceful presence. She was about my age, mid-thirties, and very pretty. Her smile was warm as she waited patiently for me to answer.

"Hi. It's a beautiful shop you have here. I think what I am looking for you don't have."

"Depends what it is." Her tone was encouraging and, feeling bold, I went on.

As I was telling her what I was looking for, she leaned toward me and motioned for me to follow. Behind a closed door, I found what I wanted.

"We don't keep this section on the floor because of its personal nature. But feel free to look around. If you find something you want, just let me know." With that she was out of the room she had taken me into.

It was brightly lit and, looking around for a bit, I found what I was looking for. Finding some accessories, I made my way out of the room. I had never done anything so bold in my life. Seeing her tidying the floor, I discussed what I wanted and she made her way back to the room. Following her, I confirmed what I wanted and she wrapped them to take them back to the floor to ring up.

Back up in my room I felt so brazen. What would John think when he came back and saw what I had purchased? He said he wanted a few hours to work out. Checking the clock, I knew he was already two and a half into it.

In the bath, I changed and pulled up my hair. The ruby diamond earrings and necklace shone brightly against my ears and throat. I applied a light amount of make-up and lip gloss. Slipping on the shoes, I tied the robe around myself and waited.

I had never worn anything like I had on now and it felt strange on my body. The shoes were awkward to walk in, but with a little concentration I knew could do it. The sun was bright on my face as I looked outside. It felt good to bask in the light.

The sound of the door opening had me pulling my robe closed and going over to the bed. John walked in looking sweaty and excited. A spring was in his step as he made his way into the room with a wide grin on his handsome face.

"Hello, Phoenix."

My husband's whole demeanor was so powerful. "How was your workout?"

Standing still for a moment, he eyed me and then turned to the bath. "I can definitely feel it. Not like what I have at our home, but it was good! Give me a few minutes and I will be right out."

The shower started and the bath didn't door didn't shut again. Would this be a habit for him? I heard the sound of the water change and John made a sound. He must be in.

Untying the robe, I laid it on the end of the bed. Housekeeping had been here and the room was tidy when I came back. I was never so glad for a clean room.

Water stopped and I heard John moving. "There are a couple of places around town, historical sites, I thought we might visit today. May require a little bit of work to get to them as they are off the path but sound intriguing." The sound of him moving out of the shower. Water running, teeth being brushed.

Trying not to break out into a sweat because I was so nervous, I waited.

Water running again and then stopping. "Then I thought we would see what else we could…" As he rounded the corner, he stopped and stared at me.

The heat came back to my cheeks as my husband's eyes traveled up and down my body. I knew what he was seeing on me and I became self-conscious. "I thought maybe I would buy something to match the earrings and necklace." They were warm as I touched them.

John's entire demeanor changed from easy to charged. His eyes a liquid steel as they met mine. A slight swipe of his tongue against his lips. The thought of being trapped came to me and I pushed it aside. This was for John as a thank you for the earrings and necklace.

"I thought you would appreciate the color. Ruby like my jewelry." I gestured to the sheer black and red cami that was split down the front and held together with a black ribbon.

His hands came to his sides and his eyes kept traveling up and down my body.

I wasn't trim. Yes, I enjoyed being active, but my five-foot-five body had never been smaller than a size twelve no matter how hard I tried. Not sure what he thinking, I went to take a step and opened my mouth to speak.

"Stop."

The command had me halting mid-step and setting down my foot. I had never heard John tell me to do anything with that voice. It was a mix of huskiness and something else.

"Phoenix, where did you get," his hand gestured up and down my body slowly and then his eyes pinned me in place, "that perfection?"

My hand came to my chest as my heart pounded. The hardness of his tone shocked me and I swallowed, hard. "There's… there's a boutique downstairs." *Did he not like it?* "I told the saleslady what I wanted and she helped me find it."

His head nodded up and down once as he stared at me. His mouth was set like he was angry and his eyes had changed to a color I had never seen. They were almost… green? How did he do that? His hands flexed and I could see the muscles shifting and bunching in his entire body. Was he angry? Why?

"I wanted to buy something that complemented the gifts you had given me. I thought you would appreciate it." Tears sprang to my eyes and I went to my suitcase.

A hand wrapped around my waist and John pulled me to his body. The towel around his waist was long and I could feel it though the lace of the cami. His breath moved across my ear and I shivered. It was hot and panting. "You're like a present. I want to take that bow tied on your chest and pull it open with my teeth."

My breath came in pants, too. I thought my heart would pound out of my chest!

"Your lips drop sweetness as the honeycomb, my bride; milk and honey are under your tongue." Turning my head with one hand, he kissed me until I had to grasp him for support to stand. His other hand trailed down the side of my body slowly. "I am faint with love."

"I..." My panting was a thing now and my body took on a life of its own. "I thought you didn't like... it." Why did I feel so close to weeping now? Not out of sadness or pain but out of the love that was overflowing in my heart for my husband.

"How beautiful you are! How could I not like the gift as delicately wrapped as you are?"

The slow sweep of the back of his fingers from my temple to chin made my eyes close and my head lean back to lie on his chest. Violently, I shivered from the feel of his body and the gentleness he gave me.

"Do you trust me?" The whispered words in my ear along with his hot breath made me moan quietly.

"Yes." The word came out in a breath so soft as it moved past my lips.

"How much do you trust me?" His hand cupped my chin and turned my head toward him. "Tell me."

At his urging my mouth opened. "Completely."

"Do you believe I would never hurt you either with my words or my body?"

Those words had me thinking. Not enough to distract me from what was happening. It was almost as if he were suggesting possibilities. Ones I didn't know about. But I knew my answer. "Yes."

Taking my shoulders in his hands, he turned me swiftly and I grabbed his shoulders for support. "Then untie the bow, Little Red."

Doing as he bid, I felt the ribbons trail down to my belly button. The cami didn't open completely. His index finger tilted my head up to meet his eyes. "You are altogether beautiful, there is no flaw in you."

His lips met mine in a bruising kiss as he dragged my body roughly to his. The hands on my shoulders were squeezing almost to the point of pain. A sigh escaped as I gave myself over to mastery of my husband's touches.

***

My eyes came open and I blinked slowly. The entire ordeal of just doing that and acknowledging that once again I was lying on top of John came to me. His arms came around me and I surrendered to the sleep that was beckoning to me.

A hand was gently stroking my hair. Fingers threading through my tresses, carefully working out the knots. My scalp stung just a little. It sparked a memory…

"I want to hold your hair. Tell before it hurts. I never want you to be in pain. Just remind you who made you feel alive again."

Blushing, I sighed happily and my body tingled in a sweet ache. Parts of me were sore and other parts of me were almost too tender. Another delicious memory…

"Who's your husband, Phoenix?"

A sigh as he held me in his arms. The bed, firm beneath us. "You are John. Always and forever."

"Kiss me, Little Red."

I surrendered myself to him again as he pulled me back down to the bed. His teeth were playful as he began covering my body in light bites.

My body had never felt as alive as it had with my husband's firm touch. I was sore and almost in pain but happy. What had happened between myself and John was more real than anything that had ever happened in my life. With John the only thing I wanted to do was take the hand that stroked my hair and kiss it. The love I felt for John even though he had been so passionate with me almost overflowed my heart.

My lips were swollen and the thought to kiss John was overwhelming. I gave it and drank from his lips and he held my head to his. I could be with

*this man a hundred years and still not get enough of
him.*

"I love you, Phoenix."

*Lying with my head on his chest, his hairs
tickling my cheek, I smiled. With every action and
word, John Westerling had shown the love he told
me he had for me. "I love you, too, John."*

Closing my eyes, loving the feel of my
husband's touch on me, I fell back asleep and began
to dream.

***

"I said get up, woman!"

*Standing up to face Charles, I resisted the urge
to cower behind the table. He had been verbally
abusing me for the last hour and I still stood. "I just
want to go to her funeral. Please."*

*He started toward me and I held my ground.
The hand that connected with my cheek caused my
lip to split and I cried out. "Don't question my
authority! I said no!"*

"But she's my mother!"

*Another connection and I grabbed the chair as
the world darkened. "I said no! I don't care who
she is! She's nothing to me!"*

*"But she's dead! Please! I want to say good-
bye!"*

*Charles' hands grabbed me and I screamed.
His eyes intended more damage.*

"Please! I only want to go to her funeral!"

"I said no!" He thrust me back against the wall and I hit my head hard against it. Crying out, I saw stars as I righted myself.

"Phoenix?"

What was that? Charles' mouth didn't move and it didn't sound like him.

"Did you hear me? Go into the kitchen and make my dinner! Now!"

My hands came to the wall to steady myself. I could feel a warm trickle in my hair and resisted the urge to check to see how bad the damage was. "I want to go to my mother's funeral! I don't want to make dinner! She was the only person kind to me…"

Charles' hands grabbed my shoulders and squeezed painfully. I cried out again as I looked into his eyes. That was a mistake. One hand connected with my other cheek while the other hand squeezed me harder. "I said no!"

"Phoenix?"

When I looked around the room, I found John by the front door. He was standing, waiting patiently with his hand out to me.

"Come here, Phoenix."

Charles still had me by the shoulders in a crushing grip. I shook my head violently. "Please. Leave." I didn't want John to see Charles brutalizing me. The embarrassment washed over me and I closed my eyes.

"My dinner! Go make it! Now!" Charles shook me and my teeth rattled.

"*Just walk away from him. Step back and you can get away from him.*" *John's ever-encouraging voice had me shaking my head.*

"*I can't...*" *Looking back at Charles, I saw the menace in his eyes.*

"*Do you trust me, Little Red?*"

My eyes found John again and I nodded my head. "*Yes.*"

"*Then just walk away from him, my love.*"

"*I can't. He has me by the shoulders and it...*" *Taking a breath, I looked to him again.* "*Leave. I don't want you to see me like this.*"

"*I love you.*"

The tenderness in his voice took my breath away. "*I love you, too.*"

"*Then come to your Big Bad. I'll keep you safe.*" *His voice was filled with love.* "*Step out of his hands. You can do this.*"

Looking to Charles again, I saw him watching me murderously.

"*You can do this. Just step around him and walk to me.*"

"*He'll hurt you. Or me. No.*" *I would give my life to keep John safe from my husband. Wait! Charles wasn't my husband anymore, was he? He was dead and I was married to John.*

"*I said make my dinner! Now! In the kitchen where you belong!*" *The rattle had my teeth shaking again. When he stopped shaking me, I looked at him in wonder. Charles was dead.*

When I took a step around him I felt one hand slip from my shoulder.

"Good girl. Come on, my love, you can do this."

Another step had me moving completely out of Charles' hands. He stood completely still and looked forward.

"Come here, Phoenix."

At John's urging, I ran to him. My arms came around him, clutching on to him for my life. The bruises and cuts healed as I held him. His hands came under me and held me against him.

"You're safe now. I have you. He can't hurt you anymore. You're mine. I love you."

I was openly sobbing against his neck now as he held me in his arms. Charles was still in the room, but I didn't care. I loved John and not Charles. John always treated me with love and respect. Charles always caused me pain.

"Can we leave? I want to put it all behind me. Please."

John turned and I heard a door open and close. I could feel the sunshine on my body and I reveled in the warmth after so much coldness.

"I just… wanted… to go… to… my momma's funeral. He wouldn't let me." Sobbing again, I felt John moving from the house.

"You want to go to her funeral. I'll take you to her funeral."

"You can't. She's dead, John. She's gone." Clutching tighter to him, I felt him hold me more securely in his arms.

"Look up."

At John's word my head came up. We were in a funeral home. So many people were there with my family and friends. My eyes came to John's. For some reason I couldn't look into them. I was still in his arms and my arms were around his neck but he had... changed.

"You said you wanted to be at her funeral. Here you are."

"I'm not..." Looking down, I saw I was dressed for a funeral. My head came up and I met his eyes but couldn't hold them. "How did you do that?"

"I love you and I want to give you what you need." His hands loosened from me and my feet touched the floor. "You need to see your mother. Go on."

My hand took his and I noticed his clothes now. A simple robe tied at the waist and leather sandals that had seen better days. His face looked different, too. "Where is John?"

"He is with us." Slowly his hand released mine. I missed his touch. With it, I hadn't remembered any of the bad parts of my life and I was filled with... love.

"Who are you?" Daring to look into his eyes, I saw compassion and hope. Every positive thing I was ever missing in my life was encompassed in those orbs.

"Why don't you go sit by the woman in black on the front row? The one with a veil over her eyes."

The urging in his voice had my feet moving. It was odd. As I moved past people no one glanced at me. No one turned to me. I stepped around people and looked back to the man who had brought me here. His smile was encouraging and I moved forward to sit with the woman.

As I did, I saw my momma's casket, a cherry wood filigreed with roses. The inside was white satin with rose petals all around the only person in my life besides John who ever loved me.

"Hello."

The voice surprised me and I looked to the woman. I couldn't tell who she was, but she seemed nice.

"Hi." Looking back to the casket and my momma, I sighed.

"She's not really there. That's just a shell of who she was."

Furrowing my eyebrows, I looked to her. "What do you mean? Her body is right there." I gestured to the casket.

"She's with them. Happy. Whole. Safe from him." The woman turned her head toward my father and brother. They were both completely drunk. Both slurring and stumbling as they moved around the funeral home.

"My father was never good to my mother."

"Or to you." The woman's head turned to me and I could imagine knowing eyes behind the veil.

"Who are you?" Leaning forward, I tried to see behind the thick veil. It was almost solid with no transparency.

"The question is, who are you?"

"What do you mean?" Sitting up straighter now, I looked to the casket at my mother's body lying so still and lonely. Momma was neither of those things.

"He was taken from you to protect you. Another was given to you to bring healing. The question you should ask yourself is who am I?"

My eyebrows furrowed. "He was taken... You mean Charles?"

The woman's head bobbed up and down. "He knows how to protect His children." Her head moved back to the man who had brought me here.

I looked back at him. He was still standing as if waiting patiently. "He?"

"He always will. He knows John is what you need. What you have always needed. He will take care of what is His."

"He will?" The smile on His face lit up the whole room.

"John would know Him. I know you do not. Your eyes are not opened." Her head turned toward me. "But they are opening and they will see Him soon."

"I can see him. He's standing right there." Gesturing toward the man, I heard the woman laugh quietly. It sounded so much like... "Your laughter. It sounds like my momma's."

"When your eyes open, you will see Him. John will help you open them."

She stood now and I did, too. "Wait! Don't go. Please."

Two men went to the woman in the veil now. "David? Jonathon?" What were John's brothers doing here?

David's smile was so much like John's. His demeanor so open and honest. He had a playful *attitude about him. "Hello, Phoenix. We are here as escort."*

Jonathon nodded his head.

"Escort? Who…" I watched the woman I had been talking to. "You're taking her, aren't you? Why?"

"Because it's time for her to go." Jonathon's voice reminded me of the warmest breeze I had ever felt. John's younger brother was more serious than David. I liked him, too, but he had an edgier attitude about him.

"Wait! Who are you?"

David and Jonathon moved to either side of the woman.

She took their arms and looked to me. "When the time is right, allow John to bring you home. He will show you who He who brought you here really is."

I threw myself into her arms and she curled around me. For the first time in a long time I felt at home. Really at home. "Please don't go."

"It's alright. He is with you and loves you."

"Can I come with you?" The begging tone in my voice was intentional. Instinctively I knew where she was going was someplace so much better than where I was.

"No. Not yet but one day. "She stepped back from me as David and Jonathon moved with her. "I love you."

"I love you, too." The man who had brought me here came to me now. "Please." Turning to him, I looked up to Him. It made my eyes hurt and I felt shame wash through me. "I want to go with her."

His head shook back and forth once.

"Please. She's all I have."

His hand pointed and I saw John and Anna. The smile on my face was almost involuntary. "John... Anna..."

"Phoenix."

"My Phee."

Feeling the urge to run to them, I held my place. Looking back at the man, I found I couldn't stand to see him too long before I had to look back to John. Now that I thought about it, both men looked very similar.

"He is mine and I am his. We know one another."

"How did you..?" Looking toward Him now, I took a step toward Him but felt John's pull and moved back toward my husband.

"Because you will be mine, too. Just like Jonathon will be."

"I don't understand." Tears sprang to my eyes. Listening to Him, I could hear such immense love flow through his words. A love I had only ever experienced with my momma and John. "Who are you?"

"You will know one day soon."

John and Anna were smiling, holding hands. Waiting on me?

"I have to go with them, don't I?" Somehow I knew my time with He who brought me here was almost over. And I mourned it.

"Yes."

"That woman." I looked to where I had seen her and John's brothers. "She was...?"

"Yes."

"Why did I see her now? Why did you let me see her and not let her stay? She was the only person who ever truly loved me."

"The only?"

My gaze found John and Anna's again. "No. Not the only. John loves me and so does Anna."

"Who do you think brought him into your life, Phoenix Halyn Westerling? Who prompted him to stop where you were and to help you? Who has been orchestrating his and your life so that at just the right time you two meet?"

"You." The breathless word had me looking at him. I could see his patient and loving smile. "But you never helped me. Not when I needed it."

"I gave you the strength to pick yourself up. I caused your wounds to heal. I brought you peace when Charles was gone and hope when he was there. I have been every positive thing in your life."

"But you could have caused him to stop when he hit me, hurt me!"

"I can't make anyone do anything, my child. I can only help those who are mine and hope those who are doing wrong make better choices. Charles' path was chosen a long time ago." His hand fell ever-so-softly on my shoulder. "I was the voice whispering in your ear when you were dating him, telling you not to stay. That he was not what you needed. But you chose him anyway, didn't you?"

"Yes." I dipped my head. He was right about everything.

"John Westerling was the husband I had in mind for you. From the beginning. He was the *husband I had hand-selected for you. You both just took different paths to meet."*

"Could you...take... those years and the pain from me?"

"Do you really want that?" His voice told me He already knew that answer.

"No. I just wish they hadn't happened." Smiling to John, I saw him reciprocate the gesture. Anna did, too.

"Why don't you go to them? I will always be with you. Closer to you very soon."

"You will never leave me?" Taking a step toward John, I still felt the pull that was He who brought me where I was.

"Never. Nor forsake you. I will always be there when you call. All you need do is ask."

"John and Anna?"

"I have been with them for a while now. They are mine and I am theirs." I could hear the smile in His voice. "Go now." His gentle coaxing had me moving forward toward the man I loved and his daughter.

'Thank you." Stopping, I turned to Him. "You brought John and Anna to me and let me see her." I looked back to where I had talked to the woman. Moving back to Him, I kissed his cheek. "I truly appreciate it."

"I know you do."

I began walking to Anna and John. My heart filled with love and happiness. They were my world.

"I will talk to you soon."

Blossom

John's arms came around me. Anna's arms clasped my legs and I closed my eyes, enjoying the feel of my new family...

Chapter 7 "Twenty Years" - Augustana

"Phoenix?" The arms under me had me coming awake. Wasn't I already in John's arms? Opening my eyes, I felt him picking me up off of the floor.

"John?"

His laughter was soft. "Who else would it be?"

"Where did he go?" The room was empty as I peered around it. No sign of the man who had been in my… dream? "It was a dream, wasn't it?"

"What was, my love?"

My feet hit the floor and I looked up to my husband. For the second time that day, he loosened the comforter from me and dropped it to the floor. "There was a… man. A good man. And you… he… helped me. Charles was… and you… he came to me. You helped me to leave Charles when he was…" I looked to my shoulders and felt my face. "You brought me to my mother's funeral and I talked with her."

John was turning on the shower. His hands drew me into it and a washrag was laid in my hands.

"David and Jonathon was there…"

"David and Jonathon? My brothers?" John's curiosity was piqued as he washed.

"Yes, he was there with this other man. At least I think he was a man." John shampooed my hair and took the washcloth. With that he began washing my body.

"How many men do you usually dream about?" His chuckle was light, but I ignored it.

"He was… beautiful, John. Love. Light. All the good things wrapped up in the form of a man. And he was so kind. I've never met anyone like him in my whole life!"

John stopped and watched me now. "What did he look like?"

My eyebrows furrowed. "I don't remember. All I remember was how his presence felt." Shaking my head, I plunged on. "He said I would be talking with him soon."

Turning to me, his gaze bore down on me. "Do you remember anything else about him?"

"No. Why?"

John looked... envious and then shrugged his shoulders. "Details in a dream are often important. I thought they may help you interpret the dream."

For some reason I didn't think he was saying what he meant.

"The important thing is that you got to see and talk with your mother." Turning off the water, he stepped out and handed me a towel. "Do you feel at peace about it now or would you like me to arrange a service for you? I could invite my family. Yours, too."

"No. Thank you. I spent quite a bit of time talking with her. It was nice and I loved the time we had." Finishing, I wrapped the towel around my body. John took my hand and we went to the bedroom. "Who do you suppose the man was in my dream? The one I thought was you? He said he knew you and that you and Anna were his."

He shrugged his shoulders as he began dressing back into the clothes he had on at breakfast. "I have a guess, but I don't know. You said he was love and light. And that you had never met anyone like him your entire life." Stopping, he watched me. "In his presence did you feel an all-encompassing love and that no matter what happened you were safe?"

"Yes!" I was dressed now. "That's exactly how I felt! It was the most brilliant feeling I have ever felt!"

He was dressed, too. Moving to me, he took my hands. Casting a glance to the bed and then back to me. "The most brilliant, huh?"

My blush was instantaneous as I bit my bottom lip. "Well, the next most brilliant feeling. That particular feeling," I looked at the bed now, "I have never experienced with any other man." My gaze met his and I realized I was a little sore in places I normally wasn't. My blush reddened.

"You are the same color as those high heels you wore this morning. Red velvet. I will never look at a cupcake or cake the same way again. In fact, I think you have entirely ruined me for cheesecake, too."

"I was just thinking of how… amorous you were when…" I giggled. "I was afraid you didn't like it."

"Oh, wife, I hated it. If you had twenty or so dozen of them I would dread coming home to you every night."

His dramatic tone made me laugh. "It would be such a burden, no?"

His hands wrapped around me and captured me to him. Looking up, I saw his eyes turn that shade of silver that meant more. "It is a burden I would gladly bear every chance I got the rest of my life." The kiss to my lips was quick. Taking my hand, he began pulling me out of the room. "We have places to be other than bed."

"You do realize you are like six inches taller than I?" His stride was lengthy at a regular pace. Right now he was walking as if the devil was after him. "I can't…"

"Then, wife," His hand swept me up, "I guess I shall have to carry you."

Getting very quiet, I said to him. "Haven't you all this time?"

"Yes. But that's what love does." His tone was serious and then he smiled. "Besides, no matter where we are, I like the feel of you in my arms." With a smile on his handsome face, he winked at me.

"I can walk." Laughing, I put my hands around his neck. "Just slow down a little."

His laughter was boisterous. "And not have the chance to carry one of the things I love in this world?" The face he made was hilarious and I laughed. "I do tend to get a head of you, but that's only because I know you can catch up."

Why did I think he wasn't talking about walking?

"You will, my love, and be even more brilliant than I can ever hope to be."

"I doubt that. You are the best possible man I have ever known." My thoughts went back to the man in my dreams. Who was he? I could be in that man's presence all day long and wished to be.

Blossom

***

We began with a walking tour of the town.
Grand old houses with rich histories. Items from the
past displayed in every room. John was a fount of
knowledge as we discussed the various things we
saw. Our hands never left one another's as we
moved from place to place.

Lunch came next. We stopped for a light one at
a local diner. There was no lingering over our meals
and soon we were on our way. Three different
nature trails, each longer than the latest and
completely different from the others, fell under our
feet. It was a little chilly out and we snuggled next
to one another as we walked.

After that was a hiking trail that was rugged.
Not too much for my masculine husband, but it was
a challenge for me. John's six-foot-one-inch frame
seemed to clear everything. I struggled a bit, but he
was always there to help me. As we finished that
trail it was almost dark.

The walk back to the inn was a long one, but I
didn't mind. It had been a good day and while I was
slightly sore from the morning, the exertions from
the day soon overtook those aches. I wasn't in any
physical pain, but I knew I had been put through
something. Intense bouts of lovemaking, nature
trails, and a hike. My body was done for the day.

John, however, looked refreshed and
invigorated. I swear he seemed like he could do it
all over again. The more our day went on, the
happier he had become. Chatty and laid back, my

husband was an intelligent conversationalist and a
brilliant listener.

"Dinner?"

We passed the dimly-lit restaurant and I looked
down at my clothes. "As tempting as it sounds, a
hot shower and something in the room sounds so
much better."

John's hand took mine when I mentioned our
room. He began moving toward it without breaking
his stride. A man on a mission was my husband.

"John?"

"You had me at 'something in the room.'" At
the elevator, he drew me close and kissed me. It was
a light kiss and I smiled up at him.

"Pretty eager for a hot shower?"

The elevator opened and he pulled me inside.
When the doors closed, he brought me to the wall.
"I'm eager, yes." His lips found mine and I sighed.
As he deepened the kiss, I drew my arms around his
neck. He was heaven… and hell. His tongue, his
hands, his body were made to be loved and for
loving someone. And I got to be that someone!

When the doors opened, he pulled me toward
our room. Once inside, we made our way to the
shower. I pulled off my boots and socks. Reaching
for the hem of my sweater, I looked to John. "Are
you not going to shower?"

He leaned back against the door frame and
crossed his arms. A smile came to his face as he
looked me over. "I want to watch you."

My hands dropped from my sweater. "Why...
why would you want to do that?" My heart began

racing as the thought of John watching me bathe came to mind.

"Because you are my wife. Because I can. And because I want to." He looked to the hem of my sweater. "Go ahead."

"Surely you…" I felt my hair. The dirt and other objects from the walks and climbs were in it. I could only guess how dirty it was. "Don't you want to get the day off of you?"

"I do." He uncrossed his ankles and then crossed them again. "More than that I want to see you bathe yourself."

"Bathe my…" I blushed. "You saw me… earlier."

"That I did." The wistful smile had me blushing redder. "And you looked more beautiful than I could ever describe."

"I just don't get why you want to see me shower." Quickly I stripped off my clothes and started the water. The water was warm as I began bathing. I could feel my husband's eyes on me. I didn't even have to turn to know that he was watching me wash my hair and my body. When I was done, I reached for the water.

"Just a moment."

John began peeling off his clothes as I stepped out of the shower. The towel was already in my hands when I felt one of his touch mine. My eyes found his. "I want to feel your hands on me."

"You want me to… wash you…?" I had never washed anyone but myself. But John had done just that. This morning when he came back and we had been together. We had showered. He had washed my hair and body. I blushed now, remembering how he took his time doing those things. "I've never washed anyone before."

His hand was hard and unyielding as he drew me back into the shower. "I help Anna bathe and shower. You will, too. You should know how to do it." He stood still. "Do you remember what I did for you this morning?"

I picked up the shampoo that smelled so much like him. After squirting some in my hands, I reached up to his head. Even on my tiptoes I couldn't reach him. "I can't…"

John was facing away from me. He bent his knees and I could reach him. His hair was already wet and running my hands through it was intimate. I took my time working the shampoo into his hair and massaging his scalp. The feel of my husband's hair in my hands was too good to not linger. Oh how I did!

"Phoenix? Are you done?" His voice came out in a deep husky tone and my toes curled.

I looked to my hands in his hair. No, I wasn't done. I wanted to keep using my fingertips to work the soap into his scalp. My hand didn't want to leave, either. I found myself slowly checking every part of his hair, not to make sure it was lathered, but because I wanted to touch him. I couldn't linger any longer and gently moved him toward the spray. He leaned back his head and I watched the water from the spray in front of him move down his back. The urge to kiss it came to me and I did. I didn't care that shampoo was moving down it. Not where I kissed it of course. Another kiss and my hands came to his hair. Leaning back just a little, I could still feel my body touching his as I rinsed the shampoo out of his hair. There was a deep richness in my voice as I spoke next. "You're done."

He palmed a washcloth and his body wash. They came to me now and I looked to them. My eyes met his and my head tilted in defiance. "No."

The look in his eyes was of hurt, but he masked it. "No?"

Throwing the washcloth to the floor, I squirted the body wash into my hands. "You want to feel my hands on you? Then I'll put my hands on you."

His grin was brighter than the lights of the bath as he turned from me. Starting with his neck, I washed just under his chin and moved down his Adam's apple. He swallowed and I felt it. Down his chest and legs then turning him as he did me I washed his back. I washed down to his fingertips. Each of his fingers received an individual wash to the fingertip. As I turned him the water raced down his front to rinse all of the soap from his body. One more turn had him rinsed on the back, too.

I turned off the water and stepped out of the shower. A towel came around me. Next, I held out my hand and John clasped it. He stepped out now and I wrapped his towel around his waist.

His hands snaked around me and pulled me to him. My arms came around him and I snuggled into his chest. The cleanliness of his body and the little hairs tickling my cheeks told me whose body it was. "Thank you. I have always wanted someone to do that… for me."

The vulnerability of his voice had me not wondering why. Instead I smiled. I had fulfilled one of John's many wishes. My soul glowed at the happiness and love I could feel radiating from my husband. If he could deal with my idiosyncrasies, then I could more than adequately handle his.

"I love doing things for Anna and for you. But it has been so long since someone has done something so nice for me." His forehead gently rested on mine and he took my hands. He closed his eyes as he brought our hands between us, holding them. "I am a selfish man, Phoenix."

My head shook back and forth. John was the exact opposite of selfishness.

"I am. There are so many things I want for Anna. Things I haven't been able to give her, but I know you can. As her mother."

Legally I wasn't her mother. Not really. I had asked John about going to court and taking the necessary legal steps, but that conversation had ended quickly with Anna's nightmare. We had rushed to help her and the conversation never picked back up.

"I have tried to be both father and mother to her for the last five years." His steel-grey eyes opened and his mouth was set in determination. "I don't have to anymore."

"No." And it was true. I loved his daughter with every fiber of my being.

"It's been hard, having to play such dual roles and its left very little time to the things I want." Bringing my hands to his lips, he kissed them tenderly. "I've given to so many so much. Asking you to do this one thing makes me feel so selfish."

"It's not selfishness. It's not. I need to learn what to do to make you happy and what things you need from this relationship. You need me to care for you. Not just tell you that I love you but to show it. But, John, I don't know how. Not the way you need." I lifted my head from his and looked into his eyes. "But I am learning and practice makes perfect." I led him to the bed and pushed him down onto it. My lips met his and I smiled. Never had I felt so bold. I threw the towel to the floor and I saw his eyes darken as he looked me over. I reveled in the appreciation he had of my body. "I say I keep practicing until I know how to care for your every need."

My husband welcomed me with open arms.

Chapter 8 "What Would You Do"- Bastille

I was a little disoriented when I opened my eyes. A man was lying partially on me and the room was pitch black. To wake him meant more pain than I already felt. Although this time I wasn't as sore as he usually left me.

The feel of the fear that coursed through my system surged my adrenaline. I saw him lying on his stomach sound asleep on the bed. He never slept in my bed. Always he came in and hurt me, then left. Why was he still here?

Stumbling to the bath, which wasn't where my bath was, I turned on the shower and stepped in. Searching for my soap and washcloth, neither one where I had left them, I began washing him off of me. I washed myself completely and then sat down to quietly cry on the shower floor.

Trying to be quiet as I felt the humiliation of him coming to my room again and hurting me in only the way he could, I let out the frustration and shame. Only when I was almost completely exhausted did I pick myself up off the floor and turn off the water. Drying my too-sensitive skin, sobbing quietly, I walked to my bedroom. It was arranged differently and I had a hard time finding the comforter. I couldn't change the sheets now as he was still lying on them. The blood would be harder to get out of them in the morning.

I leaned against the hard wall as I brought the comforter around myself. I winced at the feeling and sat in the corner, watching the bed.

He shifted a few times in the night as I watched him. Didn't he know the longer he laid there the

91

harder it was to clean the bed, the sheets? Why didn't he just leave?

In my exhaustion, sleepiness closed over me and my eyelids fell of their own accord.

***

"Wake up!"

Charles' voice reverberated through my mind and I winced in my sleep. Trying to get away from him, I pulled myself tighter into a ball.

"I said get up, woman!"

Flinching back from him as he raised his hand, preparing myself for the blow, I tensed.

"Phoenix?"

I knew that voice! My eyes searched the room as Charles pulled me from the floor to my feet. It was odd. I could feel the floor beneath them, but at the same time I didn't.

"Phoenix?"

Something warm and wet was pressed against my cheek, but I pushed at it.

"NO!"

"I came home and found dust! In my house! I told you to keep it clean!" His scoff to me was demeaning. "And you couldn't even do that right!"

His hands came around me and started dragging me with him. "What are you....? Where are you taking me?"

"To the shower. You stink and I am going to shower you like a baby!"

Gasping, I dug in my feet. I hated it when he did this to me. To him I had to be clean at all times.

*Even serving him his food I had to keep clean.
Everything in Charles' life had to be spotless. "NO!
Please!"*

*Charles let go of me and I stumbled to the
floor. I hadn't been prepared for the push toward
my shower as his hand let go of me. "Take off your
clothes."*

*"No!" The hand that smacked my face caused
a ringing to start in my ears.*

"Now! And I won't tell you again!"

*I knew what the tone in that voice threatened.
The strap! My clothes seemed to disappear. It was
strange. I felt myself taking off my clothes and
almost a slow peeling of something from me.*

"Wake up, my love."

*Who was that? Was that an angel coming to
take me home? Was this Charles' final beating he
would ever give me after I pushed him too far? Was
I going home to see my momma?*

*As I watched, although I already knew what
would happen, Charles turned on the shower. Just
the cold. I hated frozen showers! The tears fell as I
felt myself pulled toward it.*

*"Stop! No!" The water hit me and it felt like I
was taking two showers. One was warm and
welcoming. One was cold and stinging. At the same
time, I relaxed and my teeth chattered. "C-c-c-c-
cold."*

"Wake up, Phoenix."

*I knew that voice! Turning toward it, I felt
Charles' hands take me by the wrists and plunge me
under the spray. Again the sensation of taking two*

showers came to me and I marveled at the experience. How could this be happening?

"S-s-s-s-stop!" My entire body felt both freezing and soothed. No time to think as a bar of soap hit me in the side and I cried out. A washcloth was thrown at me and fell to the shower floor.

"Wash!" Charles stood and watched me as I began washing myself in the cold water. He had conditioned me to take my time as if I was showering as usual. He wanted to see me physically shaking from the freezing water falling on me. It was almost as if he needed to hear my teeth chatter. By the time I was done, my entire body was shaking and my teeth wouldn't stop chattering. My body felt like a block of ice and I could hear my heartbeat slowing. Maybe this was my death. Oddly enough, I embraced it with open arms.

The see-through towel I was given to dry off with had seen better days so many years ago. I took my time again. Charles wanted complete obedience and anything less would mean the strap.

"Get dressed! Clean the house from top to bottom! I want to be able to be served off of the floor it's so clean!"

Being summer and hot in the house, I chose a t-shirt and jeans. Charles would expect me to dress as the weather was outside.

"No socks." He leered at my toes. "I want to see your feet as you serve me."

Nodding my head, I dressed. Completely obedient to his every command.

"Wake up, Little Red."

My head lifted and I looked around yet again. John! That was John! The hands that grabbed my upper arms were biting as Charles began to draw me from the room. "NO!"

Charles didn't stop but kept pushing me forward.

"NO! I'M NOT GOING TO DO IT!"

"WOMAN, I AM NOT...!"

The kiss on my lips was gentle, but I fought it.

With my sleeping eyes, I saw Charles still holding me, in front of me. But it wasn't his lips that were against mine.

The feeling of safety and comfort came to me. My mouth opened and welcomed the one on mine. Deepening the kiss, I dragged the body kissing me to me. I didn't really care who it was. Charles had stopped hurting me. I could still feel the biting hands, but the love that the kiss contained overrode the pain.

"THAT'S IT!" *Charles' voice rang through my mind and I cried out against the lips that were on mine.*

I whimpered.

Charles was going after the belt and the one thing I was clinging on to had left me. My body was dragged with Charles.

"NO! PLEASE! NO!" *I felt myself let go and was alone again. I had fallen to the floor when he had let go of me when he went to his room to get the strap. Charles came at me now.*

"Little Red?"

That voice gave me hope. I looked to Charles as he stood threateningly over me. "You're dead! You can't hurt me!"

"This will teach you to disobey me!"

The lips met mine again and I met his kiss. When I felt the way I did, there was no Charles, no pain. Only love. Once again deepening the kiss, I drew who was kissing me to myself. I wrapped my arms, my legs around him and held on to him as he kissed me.

A hand in my hair, pulling my head back into a more plundering kiss. The arm around me was almost painful. I could feel my body readying for the next inevitable step.

When those lips drew back, I was panting. The arms left me alone and I looked around. Charles was gone and there was a man. The same one from the dream I had when I saw my mother standing in the corner. In his hands was the comforter from the bed...

Of the room I was in. I wasn't in my room anymore and was in the bedroom at the inn. As I watched, the comforter disappeared. His hands were cupped and a glowing light shown from them.

I wanted to touch that light. It seemed to radiate love and goodness. The same things I had been missing my entire life.

"Who are you?" *My soul knew that man, but I was afraid to admit it to myself.* "You were here earlier."

"It's time for you to come home, Phoenix."

"I can die?" *Oh, please, say yes!*

His head shook back and forth, but his hair never moved. "It's time for you to let go of the memories. I will help you. John will help you."

"John?" I sighed. "My husband."

"Accept this gift."

He was in front of me now. His immenseness of presence humbled me and I looked to the floor. "I have nothing to give you."

"You can give me yourself."

My eyes came up at that and met his. "What do you mean?"

"How much do you love John and Anna?"

"With my whole heart!" The words weren't a conscious choice and I looked to him. I was ready to defend them with my life if necessary.

"John has shown you who I am."

Tilting my head, I watched him. I wasn't sure what he meant.

"You know who I Am."

Nodding my head, I watched him reach out his hand. Looking at the glowing thing, I sought his eyes again. "What is that?"

"Hope. A small measure of it can spread through your life and the lives of all those around you. It is my gift to you."

Looking back at it, I reached out my hand and touched it. Warmth and love and peace flowed through me. I saw it disappear from his hand. "I won't see you again, will I?"

"No. I have fulfilled my purpose."

My eyes met his again and I looked to his robe. "I don't want to never see you again. Can I come to you?"

"Of course you can. And you will." Bending down to me, he looked into my eyes. *"We will talk soon."* Touching my head, I fell backwards and my eyes closed.

***

I could feel the bed underneath me when I awoke. My clothes were warm with fuzzy socks and John's coal black pea coat around me. We were about the same size and it fit me perfectly. I felt safe and once I smelled my husband's scent, I knew I was home.

John stood, towel wrapped firmly around his waist, his hands fisted at his sides. "Phoenix?!"

"John..." Blinking again I saw Charles. Was this a trick? Was I asleep? Awake?

He made his way toward me. "Are you awake?"

The room seemed real but so did the dream's room. "I think so. What... I don't understand... I thought I was talking to Charles. He was hurting me."

The steel was back in his eyes. His hands took my shoulders almost painfully. I whimpered.

There was a threat about him now and I shivered because of the malice that poured off his body. That malice enveloped mine, overwhelming my senses. Tears fell again, this time in fear of the man who was my husband. Never having been truly been afraid of John before, I wasn't sure what to expect.

"You called out. Screaming. You kept saying his name."

I was having a nightmare about Charles. He had made me shower and I could feel the coldness. Although now I was warming up in the warm clothes that I was dressed in. "You dressed me?"

"You were in the shower when I awoke. You were sleepwalking. The water was freezing. I had to come in and get you." He gestured to the towel around his waist. "You were shivering. I tried to warm you up."

"What?" I had sleep-walked? No…

"I'm done, Phoenix. I won't live in the shadow of your dead husband any longer." Coming over to me, he looked down to me. "I think you like it. The roughness, the pain."

"No."

"Yes. You needed it, didn't you? You thought you deserved it because it was all you ever have ever known."

My head turned away from his face at my ear. He followed after me.

"I've been so kind and gentle with you, but I don't think you really want that."

My eyes met his and I cringed at the coldness in them. His jaw was set.

"What will it take, Phoenix? To wipe away the memories of Charles?"

The lump was back in my throat. "I don't think you can."

"Are you afraid of me? Are you, Phoenix?!"

"John, please, I…"

"Do you want me to hit you?" The emotionless threat at my ear spurred me into action. I fought him, but he held me. "Is that what you want? Because I think it is."

"No, please." I knew I was begging, but John was shattering my world into tiny broken pieces. Where was the man I married?

"I could snap you like a twig." I tried to move out his arms again. "Stop it!"

I stopped. Charles' voice rang through my mind and I immediately obeyed. My eyes fell to the floor.

"How did it feel, Phoenix? When he hurt you? I want you to tell me. I want to hear it."

"He didn't care." I could hear the flatness of my voice. All strength was gone and I was completely broken again.

Moaning in fear, I tried to move again.

"I said stop!"

Immediately, I did as I was told.

"Tell me. I want to hear it from your lips."

A shaking started in my body.

"I want to know how you felt every time you had to wait on him. Every time you had to wipe up your own blood after he beat you." Silence. "Tell me!"

The shaking became worse and I could feel myself... change. Vaguely I thought this is what the caterpillar must feel like when it was trying to break out of its chrysalis.

"I said tell me!"

"I... I..."

"What? Tell me now!"

"I," gulping in a breath of air, "I…"

"Phoenix!"

I brought my fists to his chest, pummeling him. I was fighting Charles now. "I hate you! You lying, selfish, heartless bastard!"

John didn't try to defend himself as I hit him with my fists and open hand on his chest and face.

"You told me you loved me! You told me you were different! You said you would be there for me!"

I pushed my body against his at a wall. He took everything I physically did to him.

"I hate that you brought out that leather strap and beat me until I bled and passed out. I hate that you raped me! I hated waiting on you! I hated that you came home! I hated that house!"

A punch landed on his nose.

"You never even let me go to my mother's funeral! I loved her! She was the only person I ever loved that deep and I couldn't even say goodbye!" A slap that hurt my hand.

"I was so happy when you died! I hope Satan welcomed you with open arms! The deepest circle of Hell is where I hope you reside, tortured every day! You hurt me after I had to grow up with the family I had." An intense fatigue fell over me and my mind flashed in darkness. I evaded it.

His hands captured and steadied me.

"No!"

The hands let me go. I saw Charles standing in front of me, sneering. "I can't even sleep with my husband because of you! I hate you more than you will ever know!"

I struck his cheek again and it hurt my hand.

"Rot in hell!" My fingernails came at Charles now and I felt my wrists captured.

John's voice was soft as I was taken by him. "Phoenix?"

"No!" Hands came to my cheeks and my lips. I tried moving from them.

"Little Red?"

"No." The blackness reached for me again and I barely evaded it. "You'll hurt me. No."

"It's John, my love."

Arms came around me softly, but I fought them. They weren't restraining, but they weren't letting me go.

"No, John wouldn't..."

"I can't do it, Phoenix. You look at me and I know you see him. I deserve better. So do you. I'm broken, too! Catriona left me—with a daughter. I was given a little girl whose mother didn't even want her! What was I supposed to do with that loss? With the gift that was my daughter?" His eyes found mine now. "I named her Anna because it means favor. I was favored with a daughter. I may have lost my wife, but I was given a daughter. One that I could find favor in." Kneeling beside me, he pulled me to him. "I thought I could, but I can't do it anymore, Phoenix. I can't live in his shadow." His forehead dropped softly to mine. "I know he hurt you. I know you were in pain most of your marriage."

My hands were gently taken and brought around his neck. His arms came under me and I was lifted off of the floor.

"Where are you taking me?" He brought me to the other side of the room, I looked down where we had stopped.

"To bed."

Chapter 9 "The Power of Love" – Gabrielle Aplin

From the Journal of John Westerling
November 22nd
Two Days After Our Wedding

"Above all, love each other deeply, because love covers over a multitude of sins."

Before now I knew that verse but not as intimately as I do now. It's been two days since Phoenix and I said, "I do." My wife is more than I could ever hope for and more than I deserve. I thank God for her every day.

The sun has risen and if we were at home I would be downstairs with my "too-tight workout shorts" (as Phoenix calls them) on and bench pressing or curling. Glancing to the clock, I see I would be an hour into my workout already. But this morning, I am not moving. Because this morning, for the first time in my marriage, Phoenix is sleeping in the bed beside me. Her head is lying on my chest, her hand curled up in the tiny hairs on my chest. She pulls occasionally in her sleep, but I don't mind. A momentary pain for the luxury of my wife sleeping so soundly on my body.

Last night was… hard… for me. I played the part of her ex and I realize once again how much I hated him. The cruelty he displayed toward my Phoenix was worse than I knew. I could have torn that man apart with my bare hands.

I'm not quite sure how to describe it, but Phoenix looks better today. She has a glow about her that is new. I've never seen her look like this since we have been married.

She's stirring and will be awake soon. Time to wake her gently with a kiss and touch only Little Red would know from her Big Bad. This is a new experience for me.

I love my wife!

***

The warmth of the sunlight penetrated my eyelids. The sound of a book hitting a table. The feel of something moving up and down beneath my head and it was warm. Little curly hairs under my fingertips.

"Good morning, Little Red."

My husband John's voice came to me and I smiled.

"Little Red? Big Bad is going to eat you."

My eyes opened to the sight of my fingertips enjoying the feel of John Westerling under them.

"Little Red?"

My head moved on my husband's chest and I moved my nose up to his neck. Breathing in the scent that was uniquely my husband's, I sighed. This was my good husband. The one who would never hurt me. The one who would always show me love and make me smile.

Except for last night. Last night he said hard things to me. I stopped sniffing him but didn't move. They were things that hurt.

"John?" The nausea rose in my throat. "You were him."

"I know. I'm sorry."

The words that were said last night were also things that I needed to express. John allowed the blood from the already-bleeding wounds to flow over him.

He had taken everything I had given to him and still he had brought me to our bed.

The many times we had made love, I had known John was an excellent lover and we would both be thoroughly satisfied. My eyes found his again and narrowed. Something in my world was about to shift. "Is this always going to be your answer every time something happens? Taking me to bed?"

"The bed, the floor, and any hard surface that will satisfy what I have in mind." His chuckle was quiet and I saw him eye me. The steel in his eyes made them shine.

I was mesmerized by the commanding change in his demeanor. John's presence was magnetic and summoning when he was relaxed. Intent on what he wanted, he exuded a sudden danger that thrilled me. I could feel myself falling into what he wanted even before I knew what it was. It had always been like that for us. My body was more than willing to follow wherever he took me. I found myself unconsciously acting, submitting to his desires.

"I wanted to show you how a man should love a woman. And the only way I knew how to do that was take you to bed. And, if necessary, I will continue to repeat myself until you understand this is the way it is supposed to be." His lips came over mine to drink deeply of the kiss. John's head snapped back from mine and his eyes were liquid silver. "I wanted you to make love to me. John. The only husband who would give his life for you. I will ever be anything you need, anything you want."

I felt trapped in his gaze as he watched me in his arms. For this man, I would crawl through fire to do what he needed. And, in my own way, I had.

"You showed me the love you have for me."

I nodded my head, holding his gaze. My arms came around him and I kissed him.

"You showed me, Little Red." His kiss was the very definition of love. "Showed your Big Bad how much you love him. I could feel how different our lovemaking was last night. You weren't hesitant or shy with me but bold and brave." The wide smile showed his white teeth. His presence took my breath away.

He had made the sweetest love to me that I had ever experienced since we had been married. I don't know how many times I had caught myself crying last night. Not because I was afraid but because the love I felt for my husband overflowed into my eyes. And that love, that amazing love that I have for him, flowed over onto my cheeks. Many times John caught those tears with a kiss or his thumb. Did he know how my love for him had changed last night? How it had gone to a deeper level, one more intense than I have ever known? Even with Anna.

"Why do you suppose Catriona turned her back on Anna?" I looked up at him and cupped his cheek in my palm. The scratchiness of the light beard was familiar to me now. "On you?"

My shoulders were caught gently and I looked up at him. "You weren't the only one taking a chance when we got married. I was, too. I was taking a chance you weren't another Catriona. She just looked at Anna and turned her back on her. I had no one. Just me."

"I would never leave you, John! Never!"

"I know you wouldn't, Phoenix. I know." His kiss to my forehead was soft. One hand came to my hair and he stroked it. "That's one of the reasons I asked you to marry me. I knew you would stay with me no matter what happened in our marriage. I knew you would never be a Catriona."

I shivered, knowing John had a restrained power he never used with me. "About last night, what you said and did..."

"I will never do that again. Say those things to you. Never again. I just didn't know what else to say or to do."

"You said you wouldn't before…"

"I was desperate. I didn't want to be him to you anymore."

Did he realize that allowing my pain to wash over him and his to move over me bonded us even more deeply? I had no way to express the love I felt for my husband. How what he had done for me affected me so deeply. Somewhere in my soul I felt my heart capture his and connect solidly. I had never felt the depth of this love before and, in a way, it frightened me more than the fear I had for Charles. That fear was like a distant, fading memory. But this love, this connection to John was so solid, so real that it almost took my breath away.

"Phoenix?"

At his coaxing tone, my eyes found his as my fingers continued to twirl in his hair.

"When you look at me do you still see him?"

I wanted to tell him no. That when I looked at him, I just saw John Westerling. The only man I ever knew who loved me with a gentle passion and patient kindness. But that would be lying. "I don't know."

"Let's find out." His kiss was deep and skillful as he ravished my mouth.

When he drew back for air, I spoke. "Big Bad?"

With his chuckle I felt his chest moving up and down.

"I wonder. Do you intend to curl your finger in my chest hair all day?"

My eyes found my hand and I stopped the index finger from twirling in it. I didn't even realize I was doing it.

"Don't stop." His well-muscled hand covered mine softly. "I like the feel of you touching me. Of your hand on me. Especially first thing in the morning."

I swallowed. This was such a new experience for me.

His hand moved from mine and I frowned at the loss of contact. I didn't mourn it long. Sliding up his solid body, I kissed him on the lips. His eyes found mine and hardened. Almost immediately they made twin liquid pools.

"Are you tempting the Big Bad Wolf?"

A smile curved my lip and I bit it. "Maybe."

Blossom

Before I knew it, I was underneath my husband with my hands over my head in one of his. His tall body stretched out over mine, not touching me. I smiled wider and pushed the apprehension away.

"Then I shall have to show you what happens when you charm the wolf."

Letting go of my lip, I breathed. "What big eyes you have."

"The better to see you with, my love." His eyes moved up and down my body then found mine. His grin was wide and I could see his white teeth.

"What big teeth you have." I wiggled just a little underneath him. We weren't touching, but I could see a change in him. Those liquid silver eyes narrowed in on me and I felt trapped. My temperature rose.

"The better to eat you with, my dear." Bending down, he nipped at the same lip my teeth had just let go of. My toes curled. "I won't let you leap out of bed." His kiss was chaste on my cheek. "And I won't chase you." His lips warm on my other cheek and I quivered. "I think we can make better use of that energy," his eyes found mine and he growled, "can't we, Little Red?"

"I think we can, Big Bad." Pulling him to me, I opened my mouth to welcome his kiss.

***

Sliding out of bed a little later, I watched my husband sleeping. His imposing frame laying haphazardly under the sheet that had somehow stayed on the bed.

The shower was hot, which was good. My muscles were a little sore and the heat helped to work out the ache. My hair and body was washed and I was just stepping out of the shower when I saw my husband standing outside it. A towel was in his hand and a smile was on his face.

"Good morning, Phoenix."

I blushed, trying not to be embarrassed by the fact that we were both unclothed. "Good morning."

He unfolded the towel and held it open. Watching him, I stepped into it and felt it close around me. As it did, he pulled me to him. His hands went around my waist and his chin rested on my shoulder.

We stood that way for a moment and then John placed a light kiss on my shoulder. "I love you."

"I love you, too." There was a smile in my voice as I spoke.

The sudden realization that there wasn't this shadow in those words surprised me. Taking John's shoulders, I pulled back to look into his eyes.

"What is it?" His hands took my shoulders gently and he held them.

"I love you, John." Jumping up and down with excitement, I could feel the freedom in those words. "I love you!" The kiss on his lips was sound and ended with a smack!

"Phoenix?" His hands dropped from my shoulders and I pitched myself into his arms, littering his face with kisses. His beard was scratchy, but I didn't mind it now. I felt free to love the man who was my world!

Lifting my head from his, I grinned widely. My hands were still wrapped around his neck and his hands were under me. "Do you feel it?"

John's head turned quizzically and his eyebrows knitted. A grin was on his face too but he looked bewildered. "Feel what?"

Wiggling, my feet touched the floor. I took one his hands and placed it over my heart. Looking into his eyes, I bit my lip. I could taste my husband on it. "My heart." I closed my eyes savoring the feel of my husband's hand on my heart.

"You're not making any sense, Phoenix."

"It's light." I rolled my eyes. "Instead of this heavy weight, I feel…" Moving from him, I twirled in our bath. The towel billowed a little at my thighs. "I feel like I can do anything, John! I feel like I could jump to the moon or fly around the world!"

"Are you alright, my love?" John moved up to me and captured me in his arms. "I thought you were going to spin off there."

"I was probably going to!" I laughed as I felt his hand stroke down my hair. "I am so happy!" My kiss on his lips was light and I moved out of his arms. "Let's go dancing! Or sailing! I've never done that! Or we could…"

John laughed so loud, I stopped talking and stared at him. I'd never seen him so happy!

"I think my wife has finally found her joy." His arms snaked around my waist and he drew me close. "Why the change, Little Red? What's made you so happy?"

Blinking up at my husband, my hand found his chest hair and I played with it nervously. "Because I love you." My eyes met his. "When I say it now, I can feel it. Before it was like… I don't know what it was like." Moving out of his arms, I flung a hand into the air. "But now, my darling, I can feel it! And it feels wonderful!" Moving to the doorway, I looked back to my husband. "I'm going to dress and then we are going to have a day together. Just you and I." Winking at him, I walked back into the bedroom.

Going to the suitcase, I pulled one of John's shirts over my head and lay down on the bed. Shaking my head at all that had happened the last few days, I closed my eyes. Sighing, I placed my hand over my heart.

For just a moment I would close my eyes. Yes, I would just rest a moment, I thought as I felt myself drop off.

***

The feel of short hairs tickled my ear and I pushed at whatever it was that was moving across it. The sensation came again and I moaned. "Stop."

A light laugh and I frowned. "Little Red?"

"What?" I was so tired! Did this man never exhaust?

"It's nearly noon." I sat up and a slight dizziness hit me. Holding my head, I looked at John lying on the bed fully clothed. His booted feet were crossed at the ankle and his arm was crooked under his head.

"Are you alright?"

"Yeah." Slowly my eyes found the clock by the book John kept by the bed. "It is almost noon! I'm so sorry. I must have fallen asleep."

Going to stand, I felt my husband's hand snake around my waist and pull me back on the bed. I rolled over to him. He was devastatingly handsome. "Funny thing. Earlier, I came out of my shower and went to find my shirt." He eyed the one I was wearing and then looked to me. "I called for my wife only to find that she was fast asleep on our bed." His smile widened. "So I had to settle for another shirt. My wife, I thought, looks better in my shirt than I do anyway." His laugh filled the room and I smiled. "Then I thought she looked so peaceful I would just lie and watch her for a few hours. So I did."

I blushed. "You've lain here and watched me sleep?"

"I have. The privilege of watching you sleeping is one I will never take for granted. Just because you are mine doesn't mean I stop treasuring and caring for you." As he stood, my hand slipped off of his chest. Hearing a knock, he went to the door. Sitting up, I waited. He came back a few moments later with a tray. Fresh veggies and fruit, cheeses and crackers, some sparkling grape juice and a couple of small glasses were on it. He sat the tray down on the bed. "Ta-da! A light repast for you and me."

Looking at the tray and then to my husband, I shook my head. Taking his hand in one of mine, I brought my other hand to his tied-back hair. "I love you so much. You are too good to me. Better than I deserve."

His other hand came to my hair and cupped the back of my neck. "You deserve this and so much more. You are my wife, Anna's mother, and one day the mother of my child. A man couldn't ask for a wife more becoming than you."

"Before we were married I went to the doctor. I had to know what damage he inflicted on me." My eyes met his hard grey ones, his lips were set in a hard line. "Once I knew all that I would have to deal with and that I didn't have anything that would hurt you, I had all the facts I needed." My smile was a tenuous one. "I can bear a child. There was no damage surprisingly. In fact, one day I might have a child of my own… our own. I know it's a subject change…"

"So we wait and hope and pray." His words were encouraging to me and I smiled wider.

"Yeah." My hand slipped out of his and I looked to the food. "This breakfast looks amazing!" As if on cue, my stomach growled. I looked down at it and we both laughed. "I think my stomach agrees." My hand slipped into his and I looked into his soft grey eyes. It still amazed me how they changed shades like that. "Let's pray, husband. I am eager to start our day and go home and see Anna."

John watched me for a moment with a smile on his face and then bowed his head. "Dear Heavenly Father, I thank You for this day. I thank You for my wife and for our daughter. I thank You for the life You sustain us with. And, today, I thank You for the future life that Phoenix and I will create. In Your name I pray. Amen."

There was a silence as my husband looked up to me. A vulnerability was in his eyes. I couldn't help but launch myself into his lap and kiss his cheek. His arms came around me and I curled up into him. "I love you so much."

The arms tightened around me and his head softly landed on top of mine. "I love you, too, Phoenix." I heard him clear his throat as one arm let go of me. It made its way toward the tray. "Such a bountiful feast. Let's eat and then I have a surprise for you."

I lifted my head and grabbed some grapes, popping them into my mouth. Giggling, I looked at my husband. "A surprise, huh?"

John winked at me and I blushed. "Yep."

Waiting and not hearing anything forthcoming, I sighed. John could keep his secrets, I thought, finding some cheese and crackers. I smiled. So could I!

Chapter 10 "Be Still" – The Fray

John ended up taking me dress shopping. He said he wanted to take me to dinner tonight. He had already made reservations and I needed a dress for the occasion. Dresses and I do not mix. I did try to warn him of that, but he was adamant and I humored him. In the end, I tried on a crimson one-shoulder gown. John had handed it to me and I looked at it. There was no back.

"I have already thought of that. Please. Try it on for me."

Reluctantly, I tried on the dress and it was a perfect fit. Touching my back and the scars I knew would show if we went out in public, I put my hand on the door. Opening it, I felt a sparkling scarf envelope my shoulders and slide down my back. Looking up into John's eyes, I saw him wink.

"I spoke to the saleslady before you tried it on. She said it would match perfectly with this and look beautiful." He took my hands. I glowed. The scars on my back were covered and I felt gorgeous. "She was right! You do look beautiful."

Blushing, I looked at the dress and played with the pouf gathered at the side of my thigh. "It's a bit much for dinner." I eyed him. "You're not even in a suit. I would seem so out of place."

He took me in his arms and held me for a moment. "Because we haven't got around to picking it up yet."

"Yet?"

"Yes, we have an entire day ahead of us. Your dress and shoes. My suit. Dinner at…" He cleared his throat and looked at the floor. "Dinner. And then we pick up Anna from Missy."

"It just seems extravagant."

"Nothing is too extravagant for my wife. I want to show the world who she is so they can love her, too."

"How did I get so lucky with you, John?" My hand came to his face and I smiled. His head leaned into it and he sighed contentedly.

"God, my love. He brought us together. What God has joined…" His hand caught mine and he turned me. "Why don't you go change then we will look at shoes." He looked at his watch. "I will need to pick up my suit and reservations are within a few hours."

After changing, I came out of the dressing room. Shoes to match were quickly picked out. No one would ever see them so flats were a decadent luxury. Minimal accessories and soon we were on our way to pick up John's suit.

Back at the inn, I got ready as John did. He kept glancing at his watch and just as I was finishing up my makeup, he announced it was time to go. One last glance at my makeup and myself and I turned to our room. John was standing in it, midnight slacks, vest and button-down shirt. A black silk tie and a chain leading from his left pocket to one of his buttons. His dark hair was pulled back into a neat tail that slid down his neck. His facial hair was neatly trimmed and the most handsome smile was on his face. He had the most perfect mouth I had ever seen. I blushed, remembering what he could do with it.

"You look gorgeous." His smiled widened. "I especially like the blush on your cheeks. Pray tell," His arms slid around me and I looked up into his eyes, "what are you thinking?"

Clearing my throat, I smiled wider at my husband. My teeth slid over my bottom lip. "I was just thinking how handsome you are."

His smile was doubtful as was the vee that formed on his forehead. His left eyebrow dropped just a little. "Do you know what I think?"

Shaking my head, I could feel the little curls I had made brush my shoulders.

"I think you are a terrible liar." Turning me, he placed the shrug on my shoulders. "Extremely beneficial to me, not so much to you." Taking my hand he looked to me. "Have everything you need?"

"Yes." We began walking through the inn. "I wasn't lying. You are very handsome."

"I know that." He sighed dramatically and opened the door to our room. Turning to me, he took me in his arms again. "And you are the most beautiful woman on this planet right now."

Blushing, I appreciated the feel of my husband in my arms.

"Tonight is all about celebrations. We have been married three days!" He let go of me and took my hand as we stepped outside.

"There's a limo?"

He helped me in and sat down after shutting the door. The limo began moving. "Of course." His arm came around me and he slid close. He caught my hand and I turned toward him. His Adam's apple bobbed. "I love you. I love you like I have never loved anyone."

Moving my body closer to him, I sighed. "I love you, too. More than you will ever know, Big Bad."

"Oh, Little Red, I know. Because I feel it, too." His lips met mine in a lingering kiss. When our lips parted, he sat back in the seat and brought me close. "What should we name her?"

"Her?" Moving my head from his chest, I looked to my husband.

"Our daughter." He sighed and I rolled my eyes. "We could have a son, too, if you want." His mouth curled. "We should probably pick out names for a boy and a girl just in case."

"A boy and a girl. You are an optimist!"

"Realist." He captured my hand again and brought it to his chest. "From now on we talk about a child—our child—as if you were already expecting. Alright? I want to make plans for his or her delivery. Holding Anna in my arms was the best feeling I ever had next to holding your hands the day we were married." His smile became wistful. "If we talk about our child now as if you were already expecting it would almost make it real."

"What if I…"

His kiss covered my mouth and he drew back. "You will. I know. Instead of what if you can't you should ask yourself what you will do when you are. We have to talk nursery and colors and…"

"Anna! We have to have Anna with us when we talk about it." Grasping onto the daughter we shared but I wasn't the birth mother to, I knew John would stop talking. Not knowing why but the subject hurt me more than I was letting on.

"Of course, Anna! She'll be the big sister."

The car stopped and I was grateful. "I think we are here. Are you ready?"

"Phoenix? What's wrong?"

"I just don't want to get my hopes up." I sighed. "Tonight is about us, right? Just the two of us?"

John's mouth turned down as if considering my words. "Yes. Tonight is just about the two of us."

I could hear the disappointment in his voice and I hurt because I knew I put it there.

His smile picked up and he looked happy again. "Of course. Tonight is about us." Kissing me on the lips, he opened our door and helped me out. "I love you, Phoenix."

"I love you too, John."

"Let's have dinner!" Tucking my arm securely through his, we walked into the restaurant.

***

Dinner was a lavish affair with a few courses and linen napkins and China. Soft music played. Lights were low and the mood was easy. I forgot all about the conversation in the car as we ate. We were offered a Wine List but John declined. Since we had been married I hadn't seen him imbibe and there wasn't any in the refrigerator at home. I asked him if he was sure and he just shook his head, avoiding my eyes.

The limo ride back home was delightful. We talked quietly about the dinner and the restaurant, both agreeing we would go back some time. Hanging my dress in the garment bag, I ran my hand over it. I had felt like a princess in the dress and would definitely wear it again. Slipping on a pair of denim jeans and a tee, I heard John moving around the room. He had been quiet since the conversation in the car about the nursery and I wanted to talk to him about it.

Finding some socks and my shoes, I put them on. We had packed and were about ready to pick up Anna. Although he was very good-looking and took his time grooming, he was efficient. Standing, I came to him and wrapped my arms around him, laying my head on his chest.

"Thank you for tonight. It was lovely."

His arms came around me and squeezed. I loved feel of the warmth of the man who held me. "It's a possibility, Phoenix. You said it yourself. I just wanted to talk about it."

"The baby names?" I wanted a child and now I knew it was that important to John, too. "Then let's talk names."

Talking his hand, I walked us over to the bed and I sat.

John crossed his arms and looked at me seriously. "Now. You want to talk baby names now?"

"Yes." I brought my hands behind me on the bed and smiled. "Now. I was thinking if it's a girl then we should name her Sarah."

"Sarah?"

"Sarah was the mother of Isaac. She laughed when she found out she was going to have a baby. If I find out I was pregnant, I would laugh, too." Sitting up, I brought my hands together. "Sarah."

"Abigail."

"Abigail?"

"Yes." He sat down on the bed beside me, smile in place. I could tell he was relaxing. "When we first met, you reminded me of Abigail. You stayed with Charles because of your devotion. She would be named Abigail."

"A boy?" I ventured on that one already knowing the name I would choose.

"Benjamin. Good solid Bible name." He took my hands and looked into my eyes.

"Adam." I giggled. Maybe it was okay to talk possibilities.

"Why Adam?" His head turned and his left eyebrow came up.

"Because," I leaned forward, "I like kissing your Adam's apple." I did just that then leaned back. "Calling our son Adam would remind me how it feels to kiss you."

"Phoenix Westerling," his arms caught me and dragged me to him, "what am I going to do with you?"

"What would you like to do with me?" Wiggling my eyebrows suggestively, I saw him smile. I knew that smile…

"We have to check out soon. The manager extended our checkout and we can't stay another night. Anna is expecting us."

"I know. It's just nice to be able to flirt with my husband."

"And I like you flirting with me." He stood now and began picking up our things.

"John?'

"Yes?" Turning to me with a huge grin on his face, he waited.

"Last night, I saw him again. The man from my dream." My hands came together and I twisted my fingers together.

He set down our things and moved to the bed. Sitting upon it, he took my hands. "Are you sure it was the same one?"

"Yes. I know how he feels, you know?"

His head bobbed up and down once, the ponytail moving against his shoulders.

"He was standing in the corner, the one you found me in the last two nights. He had our comforter in his hands. The comforter vanished and in his hands there was a glowing."

"Glowing?"

"Yes. I didn't know what it was, only that I wanted it."

"What happened?"

"He said it was time to go home. That it was time for me to let go of the memories. And that he would help me and so would you."

"I will always help you. With anything you need."

"He held out this glowing thing and told me it was a gift and to take it. It was hope. It was his gift to me. I touched it and this... peace came over me. I knew I wouldn't see him again even though I wanted to." Taking his hands, I looked into his eyes. "I know who it was!"

"Phoenix, are you saying…"

"Yes! His presence felt exactly like I feel when you speak to him in prayer. Exactly."

"We can't see him and live."

"Really?" I would have to read his Bible more. There was not a lot I knew about it! "He said I can come to him and I want to. Right now! Can we do it right now?"

John blinked at me, disbelieving. "You want to talk to God right now?"

"Yes." I squeezed John's hands and smiled. "It's like he's prepared me to do this at this very moment!"

John's eyes filled with tears and I him smile. "I would be honored to help you meet Him." He sat up straighter and laughed quietly.

"What?" I tried to find his eyes as he watched our joined hands.

"I didn't think I would have the privilege of leading my wife to the Lord. Especially so soon." He watched me now. "Do you even know who he is?"

"Yes! And I love him! Not like I love you or Anna, but I know I love him. He said we would talk soon. Can we do that now?"

"Of course." He bowed his head and I followed. "Just repeat after me and then I promise to help guide you in your walk."

After a few short phrases, I felt a light enter my spirit and I felt… tall. Good! I felt whole and happy.

John lifted his head at the same time I did. A huge smile was on his face and he was crying. "Thank you."

"Thank you! What do I do now?"

He laughed loudly and let go of my hands. "Now, my love, we get you a Bible. If you go to Sunday school and church with us and build a relationship with him you will get to know him more and more."

"Relationship?" That sounded so weird.

"Relationship. We are married. You and Anna are mother and daughter. You feel that way in your heart toward my daughter. We have different relationships. Your relationship with Him is one that you need and that I need you to need. So does Anna."

"It just sounds weird. Relationship."

John picked up our things and we went to the lobby. After settling the bill, we were soon in the truck and on our way back home.

"You okay?" His hand was in mine and it felt so right.

"Yes. I was just thinking about a relationship with the guy from my dreams."

"I don't think it was a dream, Phoenix."

"What else would it be?" Turning to look at him, I saw him tense then relax as he drove.

"A vision. It's kind of like a dream. He came to you because you needed him."

"I asked him to take all the bad times away. He said no. It was just as well. If I didn't have them I don't think I would have met you." The kiss to my hands was unexpected and I giggled.

"Well, I for one am glad He brought me to you."

Blinking, I closed my eyes. It was late and the exhaustion, both mental and physical, from the last few days was catching up to me.

"I'll let you know when we get to Missy and Dale's."

"Yeah, I think I'm going to…" My eyelids dropped and I promptly fell asleep.

It seemed I had just closed my eyes and we were at Missy and Dale's. We thanked them for watching our Anna and brought her home. Getting her ready for bed, she yawned and yawned as we did prayers.

John took my hand and we made our way back to our room. Pulling me to our bed, we sat down. "Did you have a good nap, Little Red?"

I backed up on the bed and giggled. John followed on all fours. "You're just a patient wolf, aren't you, Big Bad?"

"You bet I am." He pounced on me and I gave up the fight, sighing blissfully.

Blossom

Chapter 11 "I Love You Always Forever" – Donna Lewis

From the Journal of John Westerling
November 23rd

Today is the first day we have as a family. I woke this morning and Phoenix was sleeping soundly beside me. My arms were around the woman I love, her curves nestled into mine, her hand on my chest. Lying there for a while, I just basked in the feeling of having a wife. It's so new.

I never felt like this with Catriona. She was always out of bed before I was, dressed and ready for the day. Lying with her, enjoying her presence was something I could never enjoy. She was always go, go, go.

In a way, after our split, I became that way, too. I was always on the go but dedicated to my daughter. She always came first. I was up with the dawn, downstairs working out before my day even began. When Anna awoke I was always there for her.

But with Phoenix in our life now, what differences will there be? I know there will be adjustments and I know God will lead us through them. Honestly, I thought about getting up this morning and going downstairs but Phoenix's warm body next to me called more. How could I leave such perfection?

She doesn't consider herself perfect, though. The scars covering so much of her body don't bother me, but they do her. I see her covering herself so much around me. She is bothered by the marks that Charles gave her, but I don't see them as

128

imperfections. I see them as badges of survival. Proof that my Phoenix has walked through the fire and has been reborn. I shall endeavor to show my Love that she need not be ashamed around me but to allow me to see her as she is. As I do now. A woman made of courage with a heart full of love.

Anna is awake! Phoenix has moved away from me in her sleep toward the edge of the bed. It is as if she is anticipating Anna even in her sleep. That means it is time for me to begin my day with my new family.

I can't wait!

***

"No!"

"Why?"

"Because it's what I want."

John threw up his hands as he looked to me. His smile was killer. It could bring me to my knees —and had—and definitely would again! "Fine. Take it."

Squealing with delight, I leaned over and kissed my husband on the cheek. His hands found my arms and pulled me closer. Before I knew it, I found myself on his lap. If Charles had used such force on me I would have cringed and tensed every muscle in my body. As it was, it was John and my body completely relaxed into his, ready for whatever he wanted.

"But there will be a price, milady. You must pay for what you want."

His tone had dropped into those low, seductive notes that made my toes curl. My eyes met his and my eyelashes batted. "And just what price would that be, sir?"

"A kiss."

His eyes found my lips as I bit my lower one. "And if I should say no?"

"Then I shall have to take it by force."

My head moved toward his. "I would like to see you try."

"Is that a challenge?" He was moving toward me, too.

"Oh, most definitely…" A smile curled my mouth as his lips descended toward mine.

"Daddy! Phee landed on Free Parking. The rules say she gets what's in the middle." Anna's voice was happy and confident.

Both daughter and daddy had already reassured me that Anna had played the game before and Anna had just proved it. That and she broke the mood for a kiss. As I began to move off of his lap, he tightened his arms around me.

"There is still the matter of price."

"A kiss, if I remember correctly." The answer came out in a breathless sigh.

"Aye." His lips touched mine and then began taking more. My hands found his face as I deepened the kiss. He was so good at doing this! Why weren't we doing this more often?

"Are we going to play?" Anna wasn't bored or unhappy. It was a child's natural curiosity. It was my Anna's voice that had me pulling myself from

John's lap. His slight, smug smile as I straightened myself had me frowning at him.

"Yes, my Anna." Sitting back down, I grabbed the cash from the middle and smiled at John. *Take that!* "Your turn."

As John grabbed the dice, I turned to Anna and held out my hands. She launched herself happily into them with a giggle. I heard the dice hit the board and leaned down to kiss the top of Anna's head. The feel of John's daughter in my arms was pure heaven and I treasured the moments I had with her.

"I love you, my Phee."

"I love you, too, my Anna."

John moved his piece and smiled at Anna. "Your turn, Love Bug."

The term of endearment he had for his daughter was cute and I loved it. The words, "Love Bug," how he had referred to his daughter since we met, were as special as Anna calling me, "My Phee." After the confrontation with her birth mother, Catriona, John's ex-wife, she became mine. As soon as Catriona renounced Anna as her daughter, in front of My Anna, in my heart the fact solidified that I was her mother now. At that point, both verbally and non-verbally, I took up the mantle of Anna's mother. And how I loved that little girl with my entire being.

Anna's little five-year-old hands picked up the dice and she rolled them. As I watched her and John count out the dots in a practiced move, I thought back to this morning.

When I had woken up, Anna was sliding in bed. The sudden realization that John and I were not dressed under the covers didn't seem to bother John. But I couldn't believe he didn't wake me. If anything to cover the scars I knew would be visible to his young daughter.

But Anna was curled with her back against me, her little hands tucked under her. I heard a sigh escape from her mouth and felt her little body completely relax against mine. In that moment, I knew I was home. With John's body curled behind me and his daughter against me, I knew a peace I'd never known.

John had prayed to begin our day. A kiss to my lips and I saw him sit up. He slid on a pair of Star Wars pajama pants and an ebony elbow-length tee with a vee in the front. Darth Maul slippers came to his feet and I looked to him. A wide grin came to him and he winked at me.

"Do you need me to…?"

"I need you to snuggle with my daughter." His kiss to me again was a lingering one. "I shall make us a breakfast and bring it in here."

"Are you sure? I can…"

"Stay exactly where you are?" He began making his way to the door. "That would be great."

He exited the bedroom and I curled next to my Anna. I had missed her. She and I had formed a connection as close as any real mother and daughter. As much as I wanted and needed time with John, I now needed the time with the little girl who possessed my heart.

"Good morning." I kissed her little cheek and heard her giggle.

"My Phee." Her little sigh was barely audible. "Why are you and daddy sleeping under the covers?"

"Because we are married." I thought for a moment. "And because God says now that we are married we can."

"Is that why you don't have pajamas on, too? Because you and daddy are married?"

Her innocent question had me blushing. I was hoping she wouldn't notice. "Yes." Looking around, I found my robe at the end of the bed. If I sat up, Anna would see my scars. "If you hand me the robe I can put it on."

"I don't want to move." She snuggled closer to me and sighed loudly.

That was just great! Hoping she wouldn't move, I sat up and grabbed my robe quickly. As it came to me, I heard Anna turn in the bed.

"Phee, why are there stripes on your back?"

It was such an innocent question. One I had tried to avoid, but now it was there. Tears sprang to my eyes. How to explain marital abuse to someone who was barely out of being a baby herself.

I slipped the robe around my shoulders quietly and moved over in the bed. My throat closed up and I looked to my hands. "Well, Anna…"

"There are a lot, Phee." She tried to look under my robe and I drew it tighter around me. I saw the hurt in her eyes along with confusion.

"I'm…" Oh, how to explain this when I didn't understand this myself. "The scars are…" Tears fell even though I tried to stop them.

Anna crawled into my lap and I drew her close to me. "Don't cry, Phee."

"Those are badges of honor, Love Bug." John came into the room and I pulled Anna closer. He had to have heard what we were talking about. "Sometimes bad things happen to very good people."

I looked up and sniffled.

"Those people wear the badges of how they survived through the fire. Then they are reborn someone new." The tray filled with our breakfasts sat at the end of the bed. John came over to us and sat down beside us. "In Greek mythology, the phoenix was a unique bird that lived in the Arabian Desert. It would burn itself on a funeral pyre and rise from the ashes with renewed youth to live through another cycle. Reborn." His arm slipped around me and I leaned into his strength. "Just like our Phee. When she and Daddy were away, she talked to God. Just like Daddy, she's a Christian."

"Phee's a Christian, Daddy?" Anna sat up and threw her arms around me excitedly. "I'm so happy for you!"

I laughed at Anna's action and wrapped my arms around her body. "Thank you."

Her laughter was music to my ears. "Daddy says when you become a Christian that God takes all of the bad stuff you did and forgets it. You become God's child just like I am Daddy's."

Anna was wiser than her five years. I had heard Pastor Brice mention something like she had said. "I guess I do."

"Jesus had stripes on his back like you do."

That statement had me stopping and looking to John.

"Jesus didn't do anything wrong and they hurt Him. But Jesus was tough! Even though they hurt Him, He still stood up to them and showed them that He was stronger. Maybe you are like Jesus, Phee!"

I felt myself blink. First John compared me to a phoenix and now his daughter compared me to the Maker of the Universe. This family truly was encouraging! "I don't think I am like Him…"

"Sure you are, my love." John's index finger under my chin had me raising my eyes to his. "He made you in His image. You are His now. He is guiding you and teaching you. I think that you are more like Him than you know."

A smile came to my lips. "I love you both so much."

We all hugged and laughed. I could feel the tears drying on my face as we held one another. It felt good to be loved.

"And I love my girls, too!" John let go of us and moved to the tray. "But I want to go downstairs for a bit before we start our day. Breakfast with my family first." He took our hands and bowed his head. Anna and I did, too. After a prayer for our breakfast, we began talking about our day.

John went down to exercise while Anna and I went to her corner to read. It seemed we had just settled in and I had just began to enjoy the feel of John's daughter in my arms when John came back into the room. We were having too much fun to stop, but John had brought a board game with him. Anna's squeal of happiness and the fact that she jumped up to run to the table told me our reading time was over.

"Monopoly? Seriously?" I glanced to Anna. "Does Anna know how to play?"

"Of course." He took my hand and we came to the table. "We've been playing for a little bit now. Teaches my Love Bug to learn to count and we have a good time, don't we?"

John bent down to his kiss his daughter's head then sat down.

"Yes, Daddy!" Anna settled in her chair at the dining room table across from me.

John sat his chair at the head of the table. I sat across from Anna. He began putting out the pieces and the game began.

"Phee?"

Anna's voice pulled me out of my musings and I smiled at her. "Hey, Sweetie."

"It's your turn."

Anna snuggled deeper into my lap and her head came to my chest. My arm came around her. It was as if it had done it her whole life. As I picked up the dice, I noticed John watching us. "What?"

"I was just thinking how right you two look together. You are her mother in every sense of the word."

I swallowed. Not every sense of the word. Not on paper, but I wouldn't mention that to him right now. "I will always be her mother. No matter what."

"I know you will." John laughed quietly as I pulled Anna closer to me, smiling as I took my turn.

***

As it turns out John and Anna never really ever finished a game of Monopoly, which was fine with me. I loved the game, but spending time with my new family was more important.

Instead, we bundled up and went for a drive. Snow began to lightly fall. It was pretty as it came to the windshield. Anna was a chatterbox, telling us what she did while we were on our honeymoon.

John and I listened intently, but I was also aware of John as he drove. He had two hands on the wheel to guide his truck through the inclement weather. I leaned back in the seat, occasionally asking or answering questions Anna would ask.

Anna was a joy and I could feel her little light shining into my soul. The happiness she exuded began to rub off on me and soon I was giggling and laughing along with her. John was, too!

Silly kids' jokes went around the cab along with questions that Anna had about where we had been and what we had been doing. I glanced to John and saw him smile at me. The blush that came to my cheeks was involuntary. John answered as I looked out the window, trying to cool myself down from the memories.

Soon Anna began to quiet and John turned the truck toward home. The snow was coming down pretty steadily now and he drove carefully. The garage door came up and he pulled in slowly.

When he turned the engine off, he looked to me. "How would you like to take Anna in?"

I suppressed a squeal. Would I? Yes! "Okay."

Sliding out of the truck, John opened Anna's door and unbuckled her. I took Anna's sleeping form in my arms. John opened the door to the house and I stepped through with her. He bent down to remove my shoes and then Anna's. I carried her to her room and laid her on the bed. I gently removed her coat and tucked the sheet around her. With a kiss to her cheek, I turned and bumped into John.

"You know for such a big guy sometimes you are sure quiet," I whispered, moving past him and to our room.

"You are so good with her." John came up and removed my coat. Taking it to the closet, I watched him hang it and then his.

"She's my daughter. Well, stepdaughter. I'm trying to show her the same love you have shown me."

Moving up to me, he brought his arms around my waist. "You've had a good teacher. Must be one of the best."

"I've never met his equal." My arms went around his neck. I almost had to be on my tiptoes, but I didn't mind. "John, I would like to be her mother in every sense of the word. I want to adopt her."

John scowled a little and then smiled. "We've talked about this before…"

My arms came from around his neck and I stood up straight. I tried to put my hands on his waist, but his hands were there. "I know we have and I…"

"Think it's the best idea you have ever had." Picking up my hands one by one, he brought each of them to his shoulders. His arms came back around my waist. A lazy smile on his handsome face. "Well, next to agreeing to be my wife and allowing me to make love to you."

A smile curved my lips. "If I remember right, I was the one making love to you."

John's self-assured sneer at me had me warming. "Would you look at that? Anna is asleep and we find ourselves with time on our hands." He brought his hands to the hem of my shirt. "Whatever will we do?"

"Every single time, huh?" My hands came to his ponytail and freed the shoulder-length tresses. I slid the ring that held his hair onto my wrist.

"My daughter wants a playmate and I want to give you what you want, too." His kiss to me was swift as his hands crept up my shirt. "And if I have to suffer through giving my girls what they want, then so be it."

I brought his head down for another kiss. "It must be so horrible being you."

"It can be." John's lips met mine and our kiss was pure magic!

Chapter 12 "Beating Heart" – Ellie Goulding

From the Journal of John Westerling
December 24th
Christmas Eve
Our First as a Family

It's been a little over a month since our wedding and Phoenix has blossomed! Sometimes it's hard to believe she is the same woman I married. She was so scared and shy; now she is more outgoing and fun. She is talking to members of our church now. Missy and she have developed a wonderful relationship on trust and mutual care for Anna. I see her hugging Anna more and being more playful with us. She is smiling and happy. Almost a completely different woman than I married. I can't get over how much she has changed!

We have begun preparing for rain—or a baby. I have seen Phoenix's reluctance in decorating the nursery, but Anna is exuberant in her planning. Anna is the one who talks Phoenix into most the purchases and into shopping for our little one. Oh, Phoenix isn't expecting yet, but when she is we will be ready. It actually surprises me, her dragging her feet on readying the nursery. She says not to get her hopes up, but I can see her looking at the room lovingly. I've actually caught her in there a few times, touching and rearranging the things. She says she's just straightening, but I know better. If the nursery was any more 'straightened' we could eat off of the changing table. And we probably already can! Phoenix insists we keep the room clean in case it's ever needed.

Blossom

The house has been decorated for Christmas. Phoenix, Anna and I have been working on decorating a little at a time and it looks like Christmas exploded in the house! This is Phoenix's first Christmas with us—first of many—and I am excited! She is, too! Right now, she and Anna are visiting with my mother, father, David—my older brother—and Evelyn, a woman with two children. We are expecting Jonathon soon but are never sure when or if he will show up.

They are thick, Phoenix and Anna, like peas in a pod. When they get their heads together, mischief for me usually follows. But I am alright with that. My girls are everything to me.

I smell pie! Warm, cinnamon, sweet apple pie! Phoenix has been baking up a storm lately and nothing in the house is safe. I'm not sure if it's the holidays or if she is just getting into the spirit. She's an excellent cook and that perfection has forced me to work out with the weights more when I am downstairs. I don't mind as long as Phoenix is happy. And I have never seen Anna so excited. Having Phoenix as a mother is exactly what she needed. Just like I needed a wife. I thought I was doing fine with Anna. And I was! But having Phoenix here, with us, makes our lives that much more perfect.

Anna is calling for me. I wanted just a moment to write down my thoughts and I had it. For Christmas I am giving Phoenix what she wanted since before we married. She's stopped asking for it and, now that it's happening, I am not sure why I haven't given in to her before. It's the best gift I could give my wife, and Anna.

Happy Christmas Eve!

***

"Lucy, you are so funny!" I laughed as John's very introverted mother told a joke that made us all laugh. Her long blonde hair and big round glasses made her look very matronly. Her small, thin stature was one of welcome and her smile was so much like John's.

"That's my girl." Edward, John's father, brought his arm around Lucy's thin shoulders and pulled her close. Eddie's voice was smooth and it was easy to see where John acquired his tone. He was definitely his father's son. "She's a crack up, isn't that right, David?"

David, John's older brother, blinked and turned his head from Evelyn and the children playing on the floor. Something told me he wasn't watching the kids. "Oh, Pa, you know my good looks and sense of humor come from mom."

Lucy blushed at the compliments she was receiving from her family. I could see now where John inherited his sense of edification. It was definitely a Westerling trait.

Eddie's laugh was deep as he guffawed with his son. His meaty hand came to smooth back his chocolate-brown feathered hair a shade lighter than John's. When he had done so, he turned to Lucy and kissed her on the lips lightly. Displays of affection must also run the family.

Blossom

Evelyn and the kids caught my attention and as I turned my head to them I noticed David had gone back to watching them again. His eyes seemed to linger on Evelyn. Was something going on between the two of them?

"Will Jonathon be here?"

The family glanced at one another at my question, but it was Lucy who answered. "Jonny comes and goes. We never really know when we will see him."

Lucy had made her way to Evelyn and sat down in the floor as she spoke. They began playing with Evelyn's one-year-old and her two-year-old. Anna was playing with them, too. David made his way over and began talking with Anna. His eyes kept coming back to Evelyn.

"I think my son has a crush."

Eddie's voice made me jump. John's silky smoothness definitely came from his father.

"I think so, too. He has been sneaking peeks at her since she arrived."

"I brought you some eggnog." Eddie's hands moved toward me with a cup in them.

"Thank you." Taking the cup from his hands, I saw his lopsided smile. When I went to take a drink, my stomach rebelled at the smell. The cup went back down. "You are all very close. Have you always been that way?"

"Yes. I have a wonderful family and I love them very much." He turned to me as I did to him. I liked Eddie. He had an open spirit that seemed to welcome anyone. "If I may say, you are different since you and my son married."

Yes, I was different. I remembered who I was when I married John and I was not the same woman. "Your son has a way of bringing out the best in people."

"I think John has a way of bringing out the best in you, my dear." He took a drink of his eggnog and sat his cup down. "Does he make you completely happy?"

My blush was instantaneous. Did he?! "Your son is the best man I have ever known, Mr. Westerling…"

"Eddie, please, or Dad. The boys call me Pa." His wink had me smiling. "I knew you were the one for him when he told us about you."

"And when did he tell you about me?" I sat my cup down.

"Sometime early last fall. He said he had met a woman over the summer, but it wasn't the right time for the two of you. His declaration of his love for you came shortly after the death of your husband."

John was in love with me all that time? I didn't realize he had cared for me that long.

"Which is why I shouldn't let my dad around my wife too long." John's arms slipped around my waist and pulled me close.

I smiled as his head rested on top of mine. "I don't know. I like your dad. We may have to talk more very soon."

John turned me in his arms. I heard Eddie chuckle and move away from us. "And I think Pa needs to think about what he says to you before he does."

144

We both laughed as did the family. They had heard John speaking and knew he was teasing me.

"I think your dad's a good one."

"You're new." My eyes swung to David. "Pa will start to wear on you after a while. He's quite the actor. Where do you think John got his mad skills?"

"Mad skills, huh?" I winked at John. "You do have some mad skills. I just wasn't aware that your family knew what those particular ones were."

They all laughed again and John mock-glared down at me. His smile came soon and he chuckled. "Those mad skills are reserved only for you, my Love."

Raising to my tiptoes, I brushed my lips across his lightly. "You are very good at what you do."

"I am." His hands came to my cheeks and he pulled me up for another kiss.

Before our lips could meet, the front door opened and a tall, dark-blonde-haired man came striding into the house. I made a beeline for Anna, but she only had eyes for the tough-looking man coming through the door.

"Uncle Jonny!" Anna ran to the man covered in black leather and silver.

John's arms came from around me and I could feel him tense. "Pa."

Eddie's arms came around me now when John's let go of me. I was pushed back behind him as John moved forward. David stood in front of Evelyn and her little ones.

Two thin but powerful arms caught Anna and held her close for just a moment. Anna snuggled into him. "I missed you, Uncle Jonny!"

"I missed you too, babe."

"Jonny." David's usually fun voice was laden with a caution. "Nice of you to make it to Christmas with family."

"Come here, Love Bug." John's tone was coaxing.

Jonathon watched John for a moment and then sat Anna down to the floor. "Better go to your dad. He and Dave have their stern faces on."

Anna giggled.

"Anna?" Holding out my hand, Anna came to me and clasped hers into mine. I brought her to my side.

David helped Evelyn gather her children and he handed Lucy the youngest one. He turned and stood shoulder-to-shoulder with John.

"Glad you could make it, bro."

Jonathon shrugged his shoulders and looked around the room. They rested on Evelyn and her children. "You've been busy, Dave." His eyes rested on me and I could see him eye me. "And yet another stunning addition to the family. Welcome."

Did all of the Westerling men have a sexy tone when they were attracted to someone? I blinked and looked to my husband. Anna was my first priority, then Evelyn's children.

John moved into his vision as I pulled Anna closer to her grandfather. If necessary I would put myself between her and her uncle. Honestly I didn't know what everyone's problem was except when he

walked through the door everyone except Lucy and
Eddie went onto high alert. John's action toward me
was new, passing me off to Eddie. If John thought
something could potentially happen, I would be
ready, too.

"See, this is why I don't make family
appearances. You guys all go from happy to openly
suspicious." He shrugged in his jacket and looked at
his brothers.

The tension in the room was thick. Evelyn's
younger child in Lucy's arms began to fuss. David's
dark eyes flickered to him and then back to
Jonathon. Lucy began to soothe him and walked
forward to her youngest son.

"We are happy you are here." Her hand came
up to his cheek and she looked up to him.

I saw his face soften as he looked at his mother.
They both shared a sweet smile.

"We were just talking and getting to know
everyone. This is Scott," her eyes flickered to the
baby in her arms and then to the woman standing
off to the side of David. "Evelyn is his mom. She is
holding Debra, we call her Debbie. Little Debbie."
Her laughter was easy as she looked back to her
son. "And you have met Phoenix, John's new wife."

Jonathon's eyes met mine and I stifled a gasp.
His chocolate-brown eyes were hypnotic, drawing
me in. He had the same magnetic intensity in them
as John's seductive grey eyes did. David's almost
ebony eyes were charismatic, too, but Jonathon's
eyes promised a danger that was very enticing. I had
to blink and look away. The Westerling men had a
rugged masculinity and charismatic charm along

with a sultry sexiness that could enslave the thoughts of the opposite sex. I clutched Anna's hand a little tighter and moved closer to her. My eyes found John and I smiled at the captivating man who was my husband. He was still tense with his hands fisted at his sides.

"Come get some eggnog and a cookie." Lucy began taking Jonathon through the room. Everyone but Eddie and I cleared a path as the two of them walked. I pulled Anna a little more between John's father and myself but she moved away from us. "Tell us how you have been. We haven't talked to you since John and Phoenix's wedding."

Jonathon's eyes caught mine again. The thought that I could be devoured by those eyes came to me. I stepped closer to Anna and drew my arms around her. She was my shield against the man whose gaze was so ensnaring. Jonathon sneered as he looked back to his mother.

"'Nog and a cookie sound wonderful, Ma." He helped himself to a cup. "Do you want one?"

"Thank you, Son." Lucy transferred Debbie to her other arm and took the cup Jonathon handed her.

John's arm slipped around my waist and I relaxed a little as my eyes met his. I drew closer to him, bringing Anna with me.

Eddie stepped forward and drew his arm around his son. "How are you doing, Jonny?"

"I'm doing okay, Pa." He eyed John and David. "Not as good as my brothers. When did you get a wife and kids, Dave?"

Evelyn blushed and David drew away from her. He had been standing close to Evelyn. "Evie is from mine and John's church. She's newly divorced and I thought she should spend her first Christmas with friends." David's eyebrows veed. "But Evelyn isn't up for discussion. Why are you here?"

"Can't a brother come back to town to spend Christmas with his family?" His eyes found me again and I looked to Anna. "Thought this should be the year I reunite with everyone. Your house looks great, John. Having such an exceptional wife suits you."

My eyes flew to Jonathon now and I took a breath. John beat me to speaking.

"Thank you. *My wife* and I thank you for the compliment you give our home."

"Relax, John. I didn't mean anything by it. Just complimenting your... home. It's lovely."

I narrowed my eyes at my husband's younger brother. "We've worked hard to decorate for the family. Feel free to look around. Our home is yours."

"That's a very open invitation, Phoenix."

"I think it's time for you to leave." John's arm came from around me and he moved forward. "That is my wife..."

"John, not now." His steel grey eyes met mine. "I can handle myself."

When I moved past John he grabbed hold of my arm. My eyes looked at his hand and then to him. For a moment our eyes clashed then he let go of my arm.

"This home is one of peace and love. I thank you for coming to visit your family, but if you are going to insinuate anything with them…"

His hands were lightning quick and grabbed my shoulders, dragging me to him. The lips that met mine weren't John's and were rough. They plundered my mouth and stole my breath from me. The stench of alcohol made me retch a little as he pulled me closer to him.

Chapter 13 "Where You Are" – Rie Sinclair

Hands grabbed me from behind and pulled me backwards. Automatically the back of my hand came to my mouth as my body met my husband's. I stared at Jonathon in disbelief.

"Out!" David's forceful tone came to me as I turned to John and buried my face in his shirt. "We tried to welcome you here…"

The bile rose in my throat and I threw myself out of John's arms. Making my way to our bathroom, I leaned over the toilet and became sick. The alcohol and taste of another man in my mouth nauseated me. As my body worked to get rid of Jonathon Westerling, I heard the door shut.

"I'm so sorry, John, I…"

"Does he know?"

Evelyn. She had come after me. I sighed and retched again.

"You didn't drink the eggnog and have been avoiding the strong smells all night."

It wasn't an accusation but a statement of facts. She was right, but I wasn't ready to admit it just yet. I shook my head.

"How long have you known?"

The water started in the sink and I felt a washcloth pressed into my hands. It was cool. With my other hand I held up two fingers.

"About right."

Her hand came to my back and rubbed it.

"It should pass but you have a bit before it does. Do you feel better or are you going to be sick again?"

I leaned back, not feeling ill any more. Gulping in a breath of air, I looked to Evelyn. "I think I am done. How did you know?"

She shrugged her shoulders. "We don't know each other well and I don't mean this in any sort of judgment, but Phoenix, you kissed Jonathon back."

My jaw dropped as I stared at her.

"John's going to ask you about it." Her eyes caught mine. "You have to know what to say."

"I didn't kiss him back!" Did I?

"Think for a minute. What happened?"

The floor was cold and stark as I looked to it. I remember being grabbed. Jonathon's mouth covering mine. "Oh my…"

"Phoenix." Her hands covered mine.

"I didn't mean…" Tears sprang to my eyes and I sat back, deflated. "I love John and I wouldn't… didn't… What did I do?"

"Eddie and David had him in the corner of your dining room when I left to check on you. Your mom had John helping her with Scott and Debbie."

I swallowed great gulps of air and looked at her. "He's everything to me. Everything! I… I love him! John's my husband… I…."

"Sometimes we don't realize what we do until we do it. You and John will talk about it."

"I don't know him. Jonathon."

"He kept watching you. As soon as he came into the room, you were his primary focus. You didn't see that?"

My head shook back and forth. "No. I didn't think of him that way."

"John tried to stop you from going over to Jonny. But you went anyway."

"I did. He was saying things about my family."

"I would have done the same thing. Would do the same thing if someone threatened my family. You should have let John take care of it."

"That seems to be a habit with me. Trying to do it all myself."

"Maybe you should let John help, Phoenix." She stood and took the washcloth from my hand. "Come on, let's go see what's going on."

I stood, physically feeling better. Mentally, I didn't know what to think.

The trip back to the living/dining area saw everyone exactly where Evelyn said they were. John watched me when I came in. He glared at Jonathon and stood.

When his hand met mine I resisted the urge to pull mine out of his grip. I thought we were at such a good place and just like that everything we had tried to work for was gone.

Quietly we moved through the hall and to our room. The door shut behind us as we sat down on the bed. John's grey eyes stared into mine. He was so quiet, his mouth set. The little dip in the middle of his upper lip was more pronounced. I had never seen him so restrained.

"I'm sorry." I tried to pull my hand out of his, but he held it tighter. "Evelyn said I... And I didn't realize it. Oh, John, I love you. It's only you."

"Did Charles ever make you do what Jonathon did?"

Blossom

The quiet anger in his tone had me stopping and looking at him.

"He made you do a lot of things. Was one of them kissing him back?"

Tears sprang to my eyes. "Yes," my voice was quiet, "I didn't want to, but I knew the consequences if I told him no." The scars on my back burned. The floor caught my attention and I stared at it. The memories of the things Charles made me do ran through my mind. So many horrible things. I thought they were buried, but they weren't.

"Then it's settled." John's resolute tone shook me to the core.

I stopped breathing, waiting for John to make his announcement. Would we split? Would I have to leave? Was our marriage over? Oh, I hoped not.

"What's settled?!" I stood up from the bed. "Because if you think that being married to a sadistic, masochist thing of a human being…"

He was up with his arms around me before I could blink. His mouth captured mine and I melted into his embrace. My hands came to his face and I pulled him closer. Our bodies met and my hands came to his chest. Of their own will they were searching the chest I knew without looking. John's entire body was mapped out in my mind so I really didn't have to see where my hands were going.

The hands that captured mine were warm and he drew back from me smiling. "That is what I didn't see when my brother kissed you. Your hands tracing what they could. You didn't react to him out of love, did you? It was out of fear. Fear that if you didn't react the way he wanted that he would hurt you."

I nodded my head, looking at our joined hands. "I didn't think. It happened so fast and I didn't think…"

"You need not fear when I am with you. I love you. Jonny's always been a scoundrel. I didn't think he would do what he did with you until I saw him grab you." His eyes hardened. "He's my brother, but I could have killed him for making you feel that way."

"He doesn't know what I endured."

He dropped my hands and ran his hand through his hair. A move so much like his father's. His eyes fell and he looked at me. "They all do. Everything I know. What I suspect you went through. They know it all."

"What?! You told them?!"

"I had to. My love for you demanded full disclosure to my family. They needed to know how to love you just like I do."

"The scars?" My skin crawled. "Did you tell them about them?"

His head shook back and forth once. "No. I thought we would tell them when you wanted to. I love you. And loving you means loving all of you."

"I just don't understand you sometimes."

He laughed loudly. "It's all guesswork on my part, my love." Capturing my hands again, he came to me. "You trust me. Don't go within five feet of him. If he can reach you, that's too close. And I will stay beside you. At all times. He won't do anything like that again."

Nodding my head, I looked him in the eyes. "I thought I could handle him. If it wasn't for the… memories, triggers, I would have been able to take care of him!"

"I bet you could have. And maybe one day you will but not now. Not until Pa and Dave talk some sense into him."

"I do love you." My hand came to his cheek and he leaned into it. His eyes fluttered closed and he smiled slightly. "It will only ever be you."

"And you are my wife. There will never be another." When his eyes opened they looked directly at me. "It's a shame my family is still here." Wistfully his eyes saw the bed and then looked back at me.

"But they are." My top teeth covered my lip and I saw his eyes drop to it.

"Still a very tempting idea…" Our eyes met and I smiled. "When we go out, until he apologizes to you or leaves, I don't want you near him. Because I will tear him apart if he touches you again!"

The restrained violence in his voice had me shivering. There was no doubt in my mind that John could do what he said he would.

"Pray."

He blinked at me.

"Let God take care of him. Just like He takes care of my past. Let Him take care of our present." Taking John's hands in mine, I came close to him and laid my head on his chest. This would be where I forever wanted to be.

His hands slipped out of mine and he drew me close. "You're right. Let's let God change his heart and mind. It may not happen tonight but I believe it will happen."

John said a prayer for the situation and for me then for himself and his family. When he finished I peered up at him.

"I love you."

"I love you, too."

His kiss to my lips was lingering and I smiled. One of his hands found mine and we made our way back into the room. Jonathon was sitting on the other side of the dining room table. Eddie and David sat next to him. John kept himself in front of me as we stopped near the table. Evelyn and Lucy were playing in Anna's corner with the two little ones.

Eddie stood and glared at Jonathon. "We've talked. Jonathon has something to say to you," his soft brown eyes met mine and then John's. "Don't you, Son?"

Jonathon's feet shuffled and he leaned back in the chair. "Yeah, Pa." He looked back to John. His eyes never looked at me. "That was a stupid move, bro. I shouldn't have done that to her or to you."

"That's right. You shouldn't have. But I still haven't heard an apology *to my wife.*" He moved closer, but I didn't. Honestly, I didn't want to be closer to Jonathon than what I had to be. When John spoke next his voice was quiet. "You knew. I told you what Phoenix had gone through. And you treated her exactly like he did. You may be my brother, but if anyone ever treats my wife the way you did, I wouldn't hesitate to tear them apart with my bare hands."

Jonathon stood. David stood.

"I just apologized to you, bro."

"But not to her. Apologize to Phoenix. And if you ever touch her again, I don't care if I have to come through Dave or Pa, you are done. No second chances, *bro*."

Jonathon blinked and looked to me. John took my hand and stood beside me. My husband's power could be quite intimidating.

"I'm sorry." His apology seemed sincere as he looked me in the eyes. Jonathon's eyes flickered to John. "I should just go. It was a mistake to come here."

Evelyn stood and made his way over to us. She took my other hand and eyed Jonathon. I saw him watch her and then drop his eyes to the table. Her hand squeezed mine and she walked over to him. I saw him turn to look at her. His chin came up and he glared down at her.

As I watched, her hand came out and cracked him across the cheek. The smack rang through the house and I gasped. The dining room was recessed and I knew the kids couldn't see what their mother did.

"You are a pig, Jonathon Westerling. If you touch any woman the way you did again I will deliver another blow across the other cheek." She stepped up to him and I saw his head drop. "I don't care where you are or who you are with. You may be handsome and think yourself a ladies' man, but that doesn't fly anywhere near me. Ever. Am I clear?"

I stepped closer to John and he drew his arm around me. We were one again.

Evelyn was a spitfire. It made me wonder what made her so tough to stand up to Jonathon like she did.

"I am sorry." He glanced at Evelyn and then back to the table. If he was five and he got in trouble doing something wrong, I am sure that is how he would have looked. "I'll leave."

"No." All eyes swung to Evelyn. "You aren't going anywhere. You are a Westerling and you are staying. If I have to sit by you all night and slap your hand or mouth I will, but I am sure it won't have to come to that, will it, Jonathon?"

Yikes! She called him Jonathon. In her mom voice. Jonathon's shoulders dropped.

"No. It won't."

What had Evelyn done? She had taken a cocky, self-assured Westerling man and pulled him down a notch. Who was this woman?

"I didn't think so." Her blue eyes met mine. "You maintain your distance from Phoenix. If I even think you are too close to her, you're done."

His head bobbed up and down.

"Good. I'm going back to my kids. Be good." With that, she turned and walked back to Scott and Debbie. Her cooing voice could be heard as I watched Dave and Pa.

Eddie's watch came up and I saw him look at it. "It's about time for presents, then I have to take Ma home. We have an hour's drive ahead of us."

Eddie drew his arm around Jonathon's shoulder. "Come on, Son. Let's have a good time tonight." He looked to John, who tensed when Eddie's eyes met his. "Alright?"

John looked to Jonathon and then back to his father. His head nodded up and down once.

"Good. It's Christmas and we're together. Let's go sing some songs." Eddie drew Jonathon over to Lucy. "Are you ready, my dear?"

Lucy nodded her head and stood. We came closer, as did Dave. He didn't look happy as Jonathon now stood by Lucy. Jonathon kept stealing glances at Lucy. His look was one of fear. Good. He deserved it.

Lucy began singing and my mouth dropped. Her simple voice was melodious and beautiful. She was a thing of majesty as she sang songs of God and Jesus and His birth. When she finished singing, she smiled at Eddie and sat down by Jonathon near the tree. He had moved over by Anna, who was talking with him.

I wasn't really sure if Anna saw what had happened earlier with Jonathon and myself. But, in her natural childlike demeanor, she had Jonathon coloring with her. What was it about Anna that just seemed to make people show love?

"You're looking at my daughter again like a mother." John's voice was a silky smoothness in my ear.

I turned to him and drew close. "She's perfect. I don't know how she does it. Brings out such love in people." My smile to him was sweet. "I think she gets it from her dad."

"My Love Bug is who she is because of God. It was nothing I did." His arms came around my waist and I drew close to him.

"You're wrong. She only shows love because that is what you have always shown her. Anna is a reflection of you."

"My wife is too kind to me. I only try to reflect my Savior. Jesus is the True Light. He is who shines through Anna."

"I don't doubt that, but it takes someone showing her Him to do what she does. I can only hope to have that same reflection one day." My head came to his solid chest and his strong arms came around me.

"You will, Phoenix. You will. And I think you will outshine the two of us."

"Alright, you two." Pa's smooth voice came to me and I looked over to him. He was standing by the tree with a present in hand. "If you would like to join us we'll open presents. You two can make me a grandbaby when we have left."

Laughter scattered around the room and I blushed.

We moved over to the Christmas tree and I sat down in an oversized chair. John sat on the arm and took my hand. I saw him look to Jonathon, who seemed to be completely avoiding us.

Eddie handed out presents and we all unwrapped them. Evelyn began to pack up the kids and to my amazement both Jonathon and David helped her with them. David carried Scott out and Jonathon carried the gifts and bags.

Both David and Jonathon came back in afterwards, saying Evelyn had left. David came to John and me and Jonathon went back to Anna.

"Ma and I are going to head home, too, Son. Thank you for having us." Eddie kissed John on the cheek, as did Lucy. He came to me and stuck out his hand.

Looking up to John's father, I found myself hugging him. I couldn't help myself. If I ever had a dad like him, I probably wouldn't be who I was today. "Thank you, Pa."

His arms stayed at his sides and he bent slightly as I hugged him. He seemed surprised that I had chosen to do so. "You are welcome, little lady. Just continue making John smile like you do. It's the best I have seen my son in a long time."

"Always and forever." The words I used with John fell from my lips as I pulled back to look at his father. "I love him."

"And he loves you."

I smiled at John. He did love me. And I didn't deserve him. "I know." My eyes found him again. "You and Ma come back soon, okay?" My arms came around the tiny woman and I held her tight. She clasped me, too, and surprised me with a kiss on my cheek.

"We will, my dear. Especially when you finally give Anna a brother or sister." Her eyes dropped to my waist. I looked to Anna.

They left shortly after and I began cleaning as the brothers talked. They all spoke quietly for a while. Jonathon gave Anna a hug and kiss and then a brief hug to John. I stayed on the other side of the dining room table. Jonathon didn't look at me before he shut the door behind him.

David talked quietly with John and I made my way to Anna. I couldn't imagine David ever doing anything bad. He and John hugged and he made his way to Anna. They hugged and he kissed her on the cheek. When he came to me, he opened his arms. Looking to John, I saw no hesitation. I walked up to David and he brought his arms around me.

"He really loves you, Phoenix," David whispered to me. "And I know you love him. Treat one another with only love and it will come back to you. Alright?"

My head nodded up and down. I moved back one foot and John caught me in his arms. "And don't be a stranger, you." I smiled automatically. "We would love to have you over when you can make it."

"This home is filled with so much love that it's almost bursting at the seams!" When he grabbed his gifts, he made his way to the door and shut it behind him.

John smiled at me and Anna. "Let's find some pajamas and settle in, family."

Chapter 14 "Like You Do" – Angel Taylor

The Christmas tree lights shone brightly in the living room. Twinkling lights that captured my attention. It wasn't Anna and my husband lying on their stomachs talking quietly, their hands fisted on their cheeks, smiles plastered on their faces. We had limited the personal presents to three each. John had been hounding me for weeks about his third present. He wanted one, but that wasn't why he kept asking. He had already bought my three and he told me he felt it was unfair that I had three while he only had two. He even went so far as to suggest that he go out and buy one for himself, address it from me, and "be surprised" Christmas day when he opened it. I knew he could play it off like he had never seen it. It wasn't that I didn't know what he wanted.

My husband's likes and dislikes weren't a mystery to me anymore. When we were married we had taken a weekend away to honeymoon. Staying close to home, we took the time to get to know one another in a way that only a husband and wife can.

As if sensing my thoughts, he turned to me and smiled widely. His hand came up and he gestured for me to join them. I wanted to, I really did, but I wanted to give him a surprise. One that I wouldn't wait to give him Christmas morning. I was too eager to wait.

Besides, John and Anna deserved more than I could ever give either one of them. They were my world now and I knew if anything ever happened to them I would not be as lost as I was before I knew the Lord.

My introduction to Him via John was a caring, kind one. He didn't preach to me out of the Bible but lived his faith. He was patient like I was beginning to know Jesus was. His life was lived in the faith I was learning to know through Jesus Christ. Leading Anna and me as he had for some time, I was sure of my decision when I had finally said yes to him. He was the Christian leader I didn't even know I had been looking for and the Christian father Anna would need growing up.

I picked up the big red bow and toyed with the edges of it. Earlier that day I went to the store to buy it. Tossing it in the cart, the cashier hadn't said a word as she rang it up. Paying for it wrapped in two bags so neither John nor Anna would see it, I brought it home and put it in our bedroom under the bed.

I remembered the first night sleeping with John. Charles had died and he knew I needed to be comforted. He lay on the covers, and I lay under them. John held me as I cried for the life that I had just lost.

The second time I slept with John, he was on top of the covers again and I was under them. I had awoken with him holding me in his arms. Anna was sleeping on the other side of me. It was the first time I felt like I was part of something other than myself.

The next time we slept together, we were husband and wife. Oh, what a night that was! I blushed, looking to the ribbon I was absently fondling. Too many near-kisses and too-close proximity led to the greatest night of my life. John hadn't stopped smiling since our marriage. If I had to find a word that described my husband it was "content."

John was content to be my husband, Anna's father, and living the life he had. Happiness seemed to course through our home and stream from one person to the other. We were not the perfect family, but love would always abound in our home.

The timer on the stove sounded and I sat the ribbon down. Standing, I saw John already at the stove, oven mitt on and pulling the deep-dish apple pie out of it. The smell hit my nose and I crinkled it. I loved the smell of deep-dish apple pie, but for now it disagreed with me.

"Thank you."

"I can't believe you wanted to make an apple pie now."

"It just sounded good." I smiled at him. "Are you complaining?"

"Never. I just fear the extra work I will have to do to get it off." He laughed and our eyes met. John's slow smile told me more than words ever could. He loved me. John Westerling loved me with a passionate, eternal love. And I knew that for the first time in my life I loved a man who stirred not only my blood but my passions. I was a very blessed lady.

He moved up to me and slowly slid his arms around me, fitting himself to me. Our curves knew one another now and we knew how to hold one another. Before it was kind of awkward and unsure. Now we knew.

Laying his head on top of mine, he sighed. The contentment I knew he felt seemed to soak into my body and I relaxed against him.

"I love you."

I could have wept at his words. They were one of the truest things I had ever known in my entire life. His love was the one thing I could always depend on. It made me hold him tighter.

"I love you, too."

Mr. Westerling. Mrs. Westerling. The words sounded and felt so odd on in my mind. They felt like they belonged there, but still they were foreign to me. I couldn't get over the fact that this man was mine. And I was his.

"Come join Anna and me in front of the tree. The pie will cool on the counter." His hand reached out and mine took it.

As he began to pull me out of the kitchen, I remembered the ribbon. I stopped, but his mass kept moving. Digging in my heels, I pulled him back.

"Wait."

Walking back, I picked up the ribbon. When I had it, we made our way to Anna, who was still watching the lights.

"Phee!"

"My Anna!" As I went lie down, a bolt of nausea caused my stomach to turn. I sat up too quickly. John's hands steadied me.

"Are you alright?" His concern had me smiling at him to reassure.

"Yes. Probably too much holiday cheer."

Anna stood and I brought her to my lap. She snuggled into me. Bringing her hand to my blouse, she laid her head on my chest. This was one of the best feelings in being a family. Well, as close as a family as we could be. Anna was still John's daughter and I was still her stepmother. A thought that had me wincing. Even though Catriona had given up all rights to Anna, she was still without a mom. And the thought tore at my heart. In all essence Anna was mine now. I tightened my arms around her as John moved next to us. His arm came around my back and his palm flattened on the floor. He had watched Anna come to me and settle. The tree had his attention now.

We sat there for a while watching the tree. Occasionally one of us would say something and laugh, but for the most part there was just a comfortable silence.

A sigh by my husband and I turned to him. Anna lifted her head from me and looked to her father.

"I suppose it's time."

Sitting on his haunches, he moved to the tree and pulled out a flat present. Looking to it, he smiled widely. His glance to Anna and then to me had me curious.

"What?"

"I was going to wait until tomorrow to give this to you, but I want you to have it now." He held out the present and I took it from him.

"Why do you want me to have it now?"

His daughter shifted in my lap and I saw him watching us. He looked nervous. "Come here, Love Bug."

As John sat down, he pulled his daughter to him. She sat down in his lap and looked at me excitedly.

"What is it, Daddy?"

John's head moved back and forth, his lips tightening even though the smile was still on them. "Phee's going to have to see for herself. I'm not telling."

I looked down at the present and then to Anna. "Should I open it? Or should I wait until tomorrow?"

Her hands clapped as she bounced in John's lap. "Now, Phee, now!"

The smile that spread across my features was natural now. I had to smile around my Anna. My eyes caught John's. "Are you sure?"

"Yes." His voice was firm and brooked no refusal.

Taking the present, I ripped the paper open and was met with a thick yellow envelope. I looked to John again. His eyes were glued to the paper. "Open it."

My hands slid across the back and I pulled the envelope open. Reaching in, I pulled out a book. My name was inscribed on the front. Phoenix Halyn Westerling. I looked to John again. "A Bible?"

"Look inside."

Opening it, I noticed a slip of paper was in front with my name on it. I sat the Bible down and unfolded the paper. Taking my time reading it, I reread it again to make sure it said what I thought it did. My eyes beheld my husband. "Are you sure?"

His head nodded up and down, the earrings glinting in the light, his short ponytail sliding over his shoulder.

I looked to Anna and smiled wider. Reading the paper for a third time, I held out my arms. She bound into them and I felt myself tear up. This was the best Christmas present I had ever been given. I held her to me tighter.

"What does it say, Phee?"

Moving her to sit back in my lap, I brought the paper out for her to see. I knew she couldn't read it, but that didn't matter. Tears were falling freely down my face and Anna was wiping them.

"Phee?"

I laughed, watching John. He looked so happy I thought he was going to burst! Holding up the paper, I pointed to the words.

"This is my name. Phoenix Halyn Westerling." I ran my fingers across the page that I just read. "And this is your name. Anna Kathern Westerling." Showing her what I just read, I looked to John then back to the paper. "This word is adoption." I began to shake as I cried and pulled Anna to me.

"Phee?"

"This paper says I get to be your mommy, my Anna! Your daddy gave me the best Christmas present I could ever ask for." I took a deep breath. "He gave me you!"

"But you're already my mommy, Phee. You said so." A confused Anna looked to me. How could I explain this to a five-year-old?

"You are so right, Sweetie. You are my Anna. But there are these things called courts. They tell adults what they can and can't do." My eyes caught John's and I smiled wider. "Your daddy went to the courts and asked them if I could legally become your mommy. You're real mommy." I looked to Anna. "And they said yes!"

"So I can call you Mommy?"

I know she had to be remembering her experience with Catriona. It was a time I wanted to take back for her. She was one hurt little girl and I was the only one who knew how to get through to her. Working with Anna also helped me. Charles had damaged my life but God, John, and Anna were the glue that put me back together.

The tears in my eyes fell for a different reason now. Anna wanted to call me Mommy!

"My Anna!" I kissed her cheek. "You can call me Mommy always! Can I...?" My eyes widened, "call you my daughter? Forever and for always?"

My heart prepared itself for a refusal. Catriona had hurt her so much. Would Anna allow me to call her daughter?

Anna stood and wrapped her arms around my neck, pulling me close. "You are my mommy and I am your daughter. Forever and always!"

"Oh, Anna!" I held her to me and cried again. The tears wouldn't seem to stop. "My daughter." Stroking the back of her hair, I heard the clock strike midnight.

Her arms left my neck and she threw herself into her daddy's arms. "It's Christmas, Daddy!" A hand reached out to me. "It's Christmas, Mommy!"

I moved over to my daughter and put my arms around her. John's arm came around us and held us. "Merry Christmas, Love Bug!"

She moved out of our arms and went to the tree.

"And Merry Christmas to you, Phoenix." Reaching over, he pulled me to him. I tilted my head to receive his kiss. A kiss I knew very well now. Ready and willing, I licked my lips and saw his eyes drop to them.

"Merry Christmas, John." Leaning toward me, I felt his chest bearing into mine.

"Daddy! Mommy!" Anna's voice had me turning. John leaned back grunting.

"We have to talk about your timing, Love Bug. Mommy and Daddy were getting ready to kiss."

"You and Mommy kiss too much!"

His head turned toward me and I blushed as he laughed. "I like kissing Mommy's... mouth very much."

Blushing redder, I ducked my head.

"It's time for the Christmas story." Anna walked over and picked up John's bible. She handed it to him and sat down in my lap. "Daddy told it last year, too!"

John mock-glared at Anna, then laughed. "We'll work on that later, I guess." Sitting down next to us, he opened his Bible.

This is the first time I would hear the Christmas story that it would mean something to me. And I would get to hear it from my husband! I pulled my daughter closer to me and put my arms around her. My chin went on her head lightly.

Looking up to us, he smiled, then dropped his head to his Bible. He must have found his spot because he started reading.

"In those days Caesar Augustus issued a decree that a census should be taken of the entire Roman world. This was the first census that took place while Quirinius was governor of Syria. And everyone went to their own town to register."

Charles had been my first husband. I didn't love him and most times I didn't even like him. He was controlling and hateful.

"So Joseph also went up from the town of Nazareth in Galilee to Judea, to Bethlehem the town of David, because he belonged to the house and line of David."

"Hi. I was just driving by. My name is John, I'm a landscape artist. I was wondering if I could help you with your yard." The memory of first meeting John flashed through my mind and I smiled.

"He went there to register with Mary, who was pledged to be married to him and was expecting a child."

"My... My... name is Phoenix."

"Phoenix? The phoenix was a unique bird that lived in the Arabian Desert. It would burn itself on a funeral pyre and rise from the ashes with renewed youth to live through another cycle. Reborn."

I gasped. Was I like that? There would be no rising from the ashes for me.

"While they were there, the time came for the baby to be born."

My eyes flew to John's and he looked at me from under his glasses.

"What is it, Phoenix?"

"Nothing." I looked to my daughter. My daughter! "I was just… thinking."

John cleared his throat. "And she gave birth to her firstborn, a son. She wrapped him in cloths and placed him in a manger, because there was no guest room available for them."

"You are always welcome and wanted, Phoenix."

"And there were shepherds living out in the fields nearby, keeping watch over their flocks at night. An angel of the Lord appeared to them, and the glory of the Lord shone around them, and they were terrified. But the angel said to them, "Do not be afraid. I bring you good news that will cause great joy for all the people."

Dale LaFevre standing at the church doors the first morning I went to John and Anna's church. "Welcome to our church."

"Today in the town of David a Savior has been born to you; he is the Messiah, the Lord. This will be a sign to you: You will find a baby wrapped in cloths and lying in a manger. Suddenly a great company of the heavenly host appeared with the angel, praising God and saying, "Glory to God in the highest heaven, and on earth peace to those on whom his favor rests." When the angels had left them and gone into heaven, the shepherds said to one another, "Let's go to Bethlehem and see this thing that has happened, which the Lord has told us about."

"Let's go home."

"Whose home?" I knew I didn't want to go back to mine. It wasn't home anymore. That house was just a place that held my things. My home was with John and Anna.

"Mine." His voice dropped. "Ours."

"So they hurried off and found Mary and Joseph, and the baby, who was lying in the manger. When they had seen him, they spread the word concerning what had been told them about this child, and all who heard it were amazed at what the shepherds said to them."

"I now pronounce you man and wife. What God has joined together let no man put asunder."

"But Mary treasured up all these things and pondered them in her heart. The shepherds returned, glorifying and praising God for all the things they had heard and seen, which were just as they had been told."

John closed his Bible and looked to me, clutching at Anna. He tapped Anna's nose, smiling. "Now it's time for bed, Love Bug." Looking to me, he said, "Mommy and I will be in to say prayers and kiss you good night."

"Okay, Daddy." Anna ran to her room and closed the door.

Turning to the Christmas tree, I began to cry softly. John's arms came around me. "Are you really alright, Phoenix?"

"I've never really heard the Christmas story like that before, John." That wasn't why I was crying. But it was the truth.

Blossom

"You have been weepy and quiet all night."
John sounded worried. There wasn't any reason to
be.

I turned in his arms and tried to compose
myself. My present wasn't going to wait until
Christmas morning, either. But I wanted Anna to be
there when I told John.

Anna's door opened and she bounded out of the
room. "Let's go, Daddy and Mommy!" Her hands
slipped into ours and we made our way to her room.

Her daddy pulled back the covers, a move I had
seen him do with me, and Anna climbed into bed.
He tucked them around her and kissed her nose.

"Mommy?"

I sat down slowly into the floor. A dizziness
overcame me now if I moved too fast. "I'm always
here, Sweetie."

"Kiss, Mommy." She moved her cheek for me
to do so.

"Always, Daughter." A tear fell and John
pulled me close to him. I had to get myself under
control. "I love you."

"I love you too, Mommy." She looked to John.
"And you too, Daddy."

Moving to her bed, I took her hand. "Do you
remember the night we were driving back from the
Renaissance festival and I told you the story of the
woman who loved the daddy and Anna?" Her head
bobbed up and down. "And I told you that Anna's
daddy and the woman got married and lived happily
ever after?" Again her head nodded. "I didn't tell
you the best part, Daughter." *Don't look at John.*
"They did live happily ever after, the daddy and

Anna and the lady, but there was someone else in the story. Can you sit up for a minute, Sweetie?"

Anna sat up and I took her hand. I placed it on my stomach. Her eyes caught mine. I heard John gasp and his knees fell to the floor. His eyes were glued to our hands. Glancing to him, I looked back at Anna.

"The woman who married Anna's daddy didn't think she could ever have a child. She was…" I swallowed loudly and John's hand covered ours. "She didn't think she could have a child. She had a cruel husband who was very mean to her."

"Like Catriona?" I winced when she spoke. She didn't call her "Mommy." I was her mommy now!

"Her husband went away. That's when she met Anna's daddy. Her daddy was very good to her. So good she saw that. When she realized she loved him, they married." This was getting too much for Anna. "Anyhow, the lady who Anna's daddy was married to, Anna's new mommy, found out she was going to have a baby."

I heard John sniffle and my other hand found his.

"She thought it was the greatest Christmas gift she could ever give Anna's daddy. A new baby, but Anna's daddy had already given the lady the best Christmas gift. A daughter. Now Anna's new mommy could give her daddy a gift, too. A baby."

"You're…?" John's voice was quiet, reverent.

"Yes. Not very far along, but this time next year, Anna's Daddy, we will have a child swaddled. A new Westerling you get to tell the Christmas story."

Anna was lost and looked to her hand.

"You're going to have a brother or sister, Sweetie!" I moved her hand over my stomach. "Still very little right now."

"A brother or sister! Oh, Mommy! This is the best Christmas gift ever! Thank you!" Anna jumped up and hugged me tight. "I'm going to be a big sister, Daddy!"

John's face was scrunched up and tears were running down his face. When he spoke his voice was filled with awe. "You sure are, Love Bug. Merry Christmas to us!"

"Merry Christmas, Daddy! Merry Christmas, Mommy!" When Anna had hugged us again, she kissed our cheeks.

I smiled. I was so happy! "Time to lie down, my darling daughter. Santa won't come if you are awake." I kissed her cheek, taking my time. "I love you."

Standing slowly, I moved to her doorway. John stood and kissed Anna's other cheek. "I love you, Love Bug."

"I love you too, Daddy."

John took my hand and didn't move as he passed me. Pulling me through the hall, he shut the door to our room. Moving me back with his body, I was pinned between him and the door. "How long have you known?"

Sucking in a breath, not afraid of my husband, I tilted my head up to look him in the eye. "I was suspicious. Confirmed it a couple of days ago."

His hand captured my wrists and pulled them above my head. "And you didn't think to tell your husband."

"You were missing a present under the tree." I arched a brow. "I can't give it to you now, but I can in about eight months."

His face moved closer to mine. "Your husband didn't need to know?"

I swallowed. "I wanted to wait and tell you Christmas Day."

"Thank you, Phoenix." His kiss on my cheek was soft. "How shall we celebrate this news?" He bent down to nuzzle my neck.

"I have ideas…" I giggled and heard him laugh.

"Don't you always?" Bringing his face to mine, he looked down to my lips.

"Kiss me, Husband. And I might tell you." It was a challenge and I knew John was always up for a challenge.

Running his tongue along the seam of his lips, he brought his hand toward me. "In the same way husbands should love their wives as their own bodies. He who loves his wife loves himself."

"Shut up and kiss me."

"Hormones already?" He tsked, oh-so-close to my lips and I smiled.

"You want to see hormones?" Grabbing his collar, I pulled him to me and wrapped my leg around his waist.

My husband gasped. "Now you are going to get it."

"Oh, please." I closed my eyes as his lips descended toward mine.

Blossom

Look forward to more of the Westerlings in
"Broken", coming May 2015.

** Cathy Jackson **
Facebook (Author):
http://www.facebook.com/CathyJacksonAuthor
Amazon: http://amzn.to/1FETc2c
Goodreads: http://bit.ly/17uBrTY
Google+: Cathy Jackson
Instagram: Cathy Redhotness Jackson
LinkedIn: Cathy Jackson
Pinterest: cathyrjackson5
Tsu: Cathy Jackson
Tumblr: cathyjackson6
Twitter: @GodsCJ

** HarshmanServices.com **
http://www.harshmanservices.com

** Videos By O. **
http://www.facebook.com/VideosByO

** Award Winning Screen Actor - John Wells **
Born in Louisville Kentucky, Wells is well acclaimed for
his dynamic versatility, expressive features, and
dramatic look.
* Facebook: http://www.facebook.com/ActorJohnWells
* Website: http://www.ActorJohnWells.com/
* IMDb: http://www.imdb.com/name/nm4323217/
* Vimeo:
http://vimeo.com/110006959

Proof

Made in the USA
Charleston, SC
04 May 2015